SO-AUQ-861

HOMECOMING

LYLE BEBENSEE
HOMECOMING

Short Stories

Third Eye
London   Canada
1993

Homecoming
© Lyle Bebensee   1993

Canadian Cataloguing in Publication Data

Bebensee, Lyle
       Homecoming

ISBN 0-919581-87-0

I. Title.

PS8553.E294H6 1993   C813'.54   C93-095055-0
PR9199.3.B42H6 1993

Published by
Third Eye Publications Inc.
31 Clarke Road
London, Ont., Canada
N5W 5W5

Dedicated to
Beth and Glen

TABLE OF CONTENTS

Homecoming

I approached the arena with a fair degree of trepidation. I had not seen some of the people who would be at the Saturday night banquet for many years.

My uneasiness increased considerably as I walked the few steps from the car to the door. Why had I come? I no longer had anything to do with religion -- yet here I was, walking with the faithful toward the huge arena. I quickly rationalized that some like me would only be there to see some old friends and find out how their lives had gone.

I was greatly worried by a particular statement on the brochure. The statement said this was to be a testimonial banquet and former members would be called upon to testify as to how the Lord had directed their lives. I hoped I would not be one of those singled out.

The first stop was the registration table, or tables, for there were two of them, and I nearly got my name entered with those of the children. With my HELLO! badge leading the way, I began to peruse the crowd, already starting to move toward the dining tables. I tried to keep the suggestion of a smile on my face -- I would be able to expand on it instantly if another face triggered my memory. I would also be a better candidate for scrutiny by those who were as reluctant, yet as eager as I was to approach a 'friendly' face. I glanced toward the door wondering if I should, after all, beat a hasty retreat. Perhaps no one had recognized me. But someone had for I was looking squarely at two friendly, smiling faces.

"I'd know you two anywhere," I called out, as we moved toward each other with arms outstretched, ready to embrace. Their eyes were the same girlish eyes of years before, and their friendliness and sparkle still sent a tingle down my spine. I wondered what my eyes were telling them!

It was a stroke of luck to run into Rachael and Lily, whom I had not seen since school days. Their warm embraces gave me security. I was not alone anymore.

"Our mother," Lily said, as she lovingly took the old lady's arm and moved her toward me. It was plain to see where the girls had gotten their good looks. I related to the gentle lady at once, and she accepted my arm for the few steps to a table near the buffet, in good view of the head table.

An ear-shattering, electronic scream greeted us from the microphone at the head table. Then a voice designed to echo across the firmament burst from the speakers, "Can you hear me?" After a moment, a crusty old gentleman fumbling with a hearing aid shot a fierce glance in the direction of the podium.

"I could hear fine until you turned on that contraption. Now I fear my eardrums will be gone for good!"

There was a scattering of subdued laughter -- the kind that suggests there should be tolerance for what crusty old men sometimes regard as legitimate remarks. A few light ha-ha's came from the local preacher at the microphone. He was due for retirement within the week and the celebrations planned for the weekend afforded him the opportunity he needed to go out in a blaze of glory.

"May God's message be comforting to your ears, Mr. Croton...and to all who suffer! That glorious message will come later from our guest speaker, the television celebrity, Clifton Hollifield." He turned his wide smile toward the evangelist and bowed from the waist. "We welcome you warmly," he said. He raised his eyes to the audience. "And to all who have come to join in this Great Reunion!"

Henry Croton, still fumbling his ear piece, looked up at the preacher suspiciously, his irritation obvious to anyone who cared to look his way. He didn't like being singled out in this large crowd of people, most of whom were strangers to him. He didn't like the hostile glances which occasionally found their target.

The preacher turned to the eleven dignitaries on his right and slowly broadcast his smile down the line, prompting appropriate responsive smiles from all in turn. Then, carrying his smile out to the crowd he announced, "The first thing we are going to do is partake of the bounty which is before you. The Lord provided the food -- that's why we are not charging you for it!" He who had become the benefactor for the Lord, now unbuttoned his rich, red jacket and pulled his six foot frame up to its full height. He swayed to the left and to the right, throwing his arms out in wide arcs to embrace the whole of the packed arena.

"Come my people," he called, "to this banquet which has been prepared for you!"

The children waited while the head table guests filled their plates. It was obviously not a time to suffer the little children to be the first in line for this blessing.

Warm, well fed bellies and the anticipation of the message by the television evangelist combined to help fill the collection plates to overflowing. When the bulging plates were placed before a neatly dressed, grey-haired, portly lady at the head table, she rose to acknowledge the bountiful offering.

"Praise the Lord!" she shouted. "P-r-a-i-s-e the Lord!" Enthusiastic applause greeted her. It ignited the zeal within her, now burning through her righteous smile as she lifted the microphone from its stand. This was the Lord's work and she was in charge!

"We have a wonderful program of music and message for you," she began. "The well-loved evangelist, Clifton Hollifield and his lovely lady who will deliver the message, have come back home! The Lord has blessed us in bringing them to us. Now...we shall have to move along in order to include all the events scheduled, for we must vacate the arena by ten o'clock. First, the message in song by the well-known artist, Roland Davenport. Roland, God bless you! Come up here and sing for us!"

Cheers rose from the audience as the young man stepped forth in his white suit and bowed deeply. "Praise the Lord!" he called, as he adjusted his electronic equipment. The Amen's were still filtering through the crowd when the stereo system sprang to life with a full orchestra to accompany the young singer. The music folded itself around us and locked us in great, encircling waves of many-decibeled stereo power as the young man raised his head, his hands and his voice to the rafters, and upward to the Lord. Religion in the pure, white-suited style of television evangelism had come to our small town reunion.

The dreaded testimonials were next. But I soon discovered that I had nothing to fear. The candidates had all been selected beforehand. It would have been too risky otherwise. The testimonials poured forth from lips and souls caught up in the magic of the colour and sound extravaganza. It was a chance for the candidates to tell the great gathering about how the Lord had guided their every move. It would have been better if the Lord had blessed some of them with a desire to learn some proper English, I thought.

As the testimonial revelations continued to pour from excited throats, and the head table guests sat basking in the glory of the moment, the grey-haired lady in charge of the program kept glancing nervously at her watch. Finally she rose.

"I regret that we have no more time for this item on our program," she announced.

The three candidates who were excluded; a young girl of fourteen sitting nervously on the edge of her seat, an elderly man whose wife was already standing, her hands clutching his coat sleeve to raise him up and a plump, middle-aged lady, her face red, her wide, blue eyes mirroring the vision of which she was a part, all sank slowly back into their chairs. The proclamation had cast a sad glow over their faces and damped the spiritual fire within their souls. The low sighs of disappointment of those in the audience who had been caught up in the euphoric moment soon became inaudible. Their eyes were now focussed on the head table and on the church dignitary whose job it was to bring official greetings from the head office.

The well-fed dignitary looked to be a man well satisfied with his work. One might be forgiven for thinking that there was, in his demeanour, some suggestion that he was very well satisfied with himself. He started with a story. It involved two old ladies, one of whom, being an ardent bowler, was worried that there might not be bowling in heaven. By some mysterious means, the other lady, in a state of extreme illness had had a short preview of heaven. When she recovered she was questioned as to whether there was bowling in heaven. She replied, "I have some good news, and some bad news. The good news is that there is bowling in heaven!" The ardent bowler beamed with satisfaction at the confirmation. "The bad news is," her friend continued, "you are scheduled to play next week!"

There was a light scattering of subdued laughter, but it died quickly as the realization swept over the crowd that there were several very old ladies present. I felt uneasy and embarrassed. I swung my eyes in a quick glance to the mother of Rachael and Lily beside me. She did not seem greatly bothered. The expression on her face seemed to reflect a kind of tolerance for such bad taste, even on the part of one whose religious politics had elevated him to a position of eminence far above the lowly flock.

"A preoccupation with the fear of death? A bit insecure wouldn't you say?" Lily ventured.

"An excellent analysis," I replied, glad to have had her speak first and confirm that we were of the same mind.

Clifton Hollifield sat with a permanent, fixed smile, resplendent in his royal blue silk suit, appropriately adorned with a white carnation. Beside him was his wife, wearing the same brand of clean, quiet smile under her television-red hair. They were both having some difficulty maintaining their composure as they watched the evening being worn away on the endless list of program activities. With but a half hour left, the coordinator continued to drone on. She seemed unwilling to risk being overshadowed by the evangelist when it came his turn. Finally, when the anxiety of the audience was becoming obvious to everyone, she relinquished the podium and moved to her place with the select few. Clifton Hollifield rose slowly and turned toward the woman who by now had squeezed her buttocks into a chair next to the official greeter from the church's head office. His eyes narrowed to slits and his face froze in a cynical smile as he focussed hard upon her for a moment. She smiled back at him as if to say, "Now go to it, big shot. Let's see what you can do with the eight minutes I have allotted to you!"

"He's thinking, 'I'd like to kick you right where you sit down!'" I whispered to Rachael. She caught herself just before her laugh escaped to the audience.

The evangelist put his Bible on the podium and looked out across the crowd. "I have come back to my roots," he said humbly. "My Lord has asked me to come back and tell you what his plans are...for you!"

Silence fell over the people. Was it possible that one of their own had been chosen to disclose the Lord's plans? Some looked at him, their eyes eager with anticipation, anxious to hear first hand what God had in store for them. Others looked worried.

"He wants you in his house of many mansions!" the evangelist proclaimed, his eyes scanning the wide arena. Lily looked at me reassuringly and winked, acknowledging that we were included. "But first you must do his will!"

"I knew there'd be a price tag," I whispered to Rachael. She bubbled into an explosive laugh before she could restrain herself. The admonishing looks on the faces turned toward us told us that we had better watch it! I avoided making any further remarks to Rachael. As a girl, she had always had a spontaneous reaction to anything remotely funny. The years had not taken that from her.

"The expansion plan needs your gifts and we have been shown a way to add this jewel to the Crown. God came to me in a dream. He asked me to share your gifts to my Television Productions...ah...Television Ministry -- those wonderful gifts which make it possible to continue this important work. God bless you! He has asked me to contribute to your local building program over the next two years." He paused briefly. The assembly leaned forward, anxiously awaiting his next words.

"I have agreed!"

Noisy applause and cheering greeted his decision. He threw his head high and in a magnanimous gesture he let his arms encompass the whole of the congregation. Then came the rhetorical question.

"And the people said?"

"Amen!" they shouted.

"We are building here for eternity. It will take time. Rome wasn't built in a day!" he mused.

"That's because I wasn't the engineer on that job!" Henry Croton said to his wife, a mischievous smile curling his cheek as he nudged her arm.

His remark, much sharper than he had imagined, had found a silent spot in the evangelist's address and carried across the arena. There was still a little of the piercing quality in Henry Croton's speech left over from the days when his voice carried commands across the construction sites of some of the world's great hydro projects.

"Praise the Lord for men like Mr. Croton!" the evangelist snapped. "Even in his ailing years he can still be counted on for a 'constructive' contribution!"

The evangelist's remark might have had something to do with the fact that he had never seen Henry Croton's name on any of the cheques which kept arriving at his Production Studios. Whatever the reason, it was interpreted by some as a punishing and distasteful blow to the old engineer. And some were glad that Henry had scored first. However, there were those who had never been able to compete with Henry Croton and who could not even now in his eighty-seventh year. Some of them would have been pleased to see the old man promptly dispatched in the direction of hell. There was no doubt that the big shot from Toronto had the stage and the limelight, but Henry Croton had a limelight of his own and it still glowed. Henry had built his limelight -- had built it into himself. It reflected through his talk, across the years of experience. He had no need for the superficial limelight of privileged officialdom. He looked up at the evangelist, his face revealing a steady, sure sense of his own worth. It was obvious to those who were watching that the evangelist did not care to face the stinging truth in Henry Croton's eyes.

"I know that you will go on building where others have left off," the evangelist continued. "My work here is done. Yours is just beginning!" Then the question.

"And the people said?"

"Amen," they roared, and the lines of the old hymn, 'There is Power, Power, Power in the Blood' rang to the rafters.

There is power in more than the blood, I thought!

On Sunday morning the crowds were already gathering as I walked toward the church. The warmth of June had blessed the flowering bushes at the church doors, bringing forth delicate perfumes which drifted intoxicatingly into the nostrils. Inside, the church was ablaze with flowers and decorations. Television cameras were in place. The choir loft which I had known so well, was now flanked by an ornate pulpit. A row of deacons -- some hellions now gone straight -- sat back where the old baptismal font had been the scene of so many torturous near-drownings. Below was the piano in its proper place. It had been joined by an expensive electronic organ, given centre place directly below the pulpit. Seated at the organ was a clean-cut, young man neatly attired in a white suit and sporting a red carnation. He looked over the piano where a beautiful young woman waited for his signal. At a nod of his head four hands pounced on keyboards to roll out music for old time religion and new time religion, to please old hearts and new hearts.

Buoyed up on the music the preacher sprang from his chair and threw his instant smile to the congregation. This was to be his last anniversary service and he would make the best of it. He stood for a few moments basking in the beauty and glory surrounding him. Then a strange melancholy crept into his smile. He seemed stunned for a moment, unable to go on. One sensed that he might have suddenly become acutely aware that his days of glory were coming to an end. He cast his eyes back and forth across the ceiling at the rear of the church several times, then dropped them to the congregation. He began to speak, but his voice was sober and without vibrancy.

"Congratulations to all those who have determined that neither age nor infirmity would be suffient to keep them from the Lord's house on this special day. Praise the Lord for their presence! Praise the Lord for the bequests of the departed! Their gifts have decorated this beautiful sanctuary. Praise the Lord for your generous gifts to our expansion program!" He had started the expansion program and he would be remembered for its success or failure.

"And now, it is my privilege to welcome our guest speaker," the preacher said. "We are blessed in having Reverend Crane to bring the message on this beautiful morning. He also has come home to be with us!"

Richard Crane rose and approached the pulpit. His attempt at a smile was a failure. No smile could cut through the stern lines of his grey face and get by the fierce coldness of his eyes. He immediately got down to the business at hand; either repent, or suffer the damnation of God's wrath in eternal hell. Of course, if you did repent and choose to be born again, the slate would be wiped clean. To emphasize the point, he gave examples in which he had been instrumental in snatching various poor souls from the jaws of hell at the last minute. One was a badly-crippled woman whom they had to baptize in her wheel chair. It had taken four stalwart men to do it.

"I had her funeral," Richard Crane said. He went on to tell of a drunken wife-beater who in the last minutes had found the Lord.

"I had his funeral," he said, pausing for the message to sink in, as he looked straight out at the congregation.

Some of the very old, eyes now fierce in deep sockets, time-robbed of the warm glow of earlier years, sat rigid and cold in the steadfastness of their faith. Some with warm eyes, in pleasant faces which had always been theirs, reflected a kind of inner peace. Their ears had never heard the roaring fires of hell.

It was the children I found myself being concerned about. The hell-fire and brimstone, which had so terrified me as a child, was still spewing from the pulpit. For a few terrible seconds I could again feel the scorching, red flames leaping up from the steaming, grey pit into which I was being cast -- 'Suffer the little children'.

After half an hour in which there was no reference made to the joys of heaven, but only to the horrors of hell, the preacher's voice was becoming hoarse, making it all the more threatening. He continued to call to sinners to repent, confess their sins and be born again.

"Our time on earth is short," he cautioned loudly. "Can anyone say that you will be here tomorrow?"

"We will if he keeps on talking!" Henry Croton suggested to his wife, his increasing irritation apparent only to those close by.

The preacher picked up his Bible and stepped out in front of the pulpit. "The Lord is calling you," he warned. "Pray now while there is still time! Surrender your life to the Lord! Come while he is listening -- he is waiting for you. The Lord is near at this moment!" He lifted his eyes upward and called, "Oh Lord, come into our hearts and wash away our sins!"

A frail old man who awoke from his half-slumber just in time to hear that the Lord was near, jumped to his feet, and throwing his arms to the ceiling he let loose a high-pitched, icy cry, "Lord, come through the roof and I'll pay for getting it fixed!" His wife took a pill from her purse and popped it into his mouth. Soon his head was on her shoulder, and he was asleep.

The preacher stepped back, leaning one hand against the pulpit. He breathed heavily; perspiration rolled off his grey forehead past icy eyes fixed in rigid stare and down his bony cheeks to firmly set jaws. His clenched right hand held the Bible high above his head. He seemed frozen in bewilderment, his zeal pressing him on to greater action; his exhaustion ruling against it. I thought of the Bible in his hand being the same book the Zealots held when they burned the Salem witches in their march for the Lord. Suddenly the old words 'Onward Christian soldiers... marching as to war' took on new meaning. The lively old hymn I loved singing as a child now had ominous and frightening implications. I looked again at the preacher. I sensed at that moment that he might be prepared to kill for the faith. I thought of the religious wars with which history is riddled.

The choir rose. The Lord's taste in music had changed since the days when I had strained to reach top tenor notes. The stolen glances between two young men in the choir and three young ladies in the front pew, dressed in bright summer frocks which clung closely to their maidenly forms, suggested to me that nature was driving home a message far more intense than that from the pulpit. It seemed to me the assumption that the flesh was evil might be posing some difficulty for most of them.

The retiring preacher stood up and swept his instant smile over the congregation. "And the people said?"

"Amen!" they chorused.

All that remained was the communion and on this special day the children were allowed to stay. As nervous fingers curled around the miniature glasses and moved them upward toward dry mouths, the preacher related the cubes of bread and the red liquid to the flesh and blood of Christ. A small girl in front of me turned to her mother with an unbelieving look of horror on her young face. "E-E-E-Yuk!" she shrieked. The mother quickly shushed the child, then sent her to the basement nursery.

Some let the red juice touch their lips. Some however, stopped with the glasses at their lips, then lowered them to the holding shelves untouched.

The food was again provided by the Lord. I took my plate to a table under the trees. A sense of well-being came over me as the food and hot coffee started to reach my worried stomach. A few old friends came by to shake my hand, then went on their way. Suddenly the crowds had thinned. I sat down under a large maple where some young children, completely oblivious to my presence, screamed their joyful sounds in the chase around and around the tree. A wave of nostalgia struck me and for a few moments I felt helplessly inundated. Desperately I wished for someone to share the nostalgia with me. But Lily and Rachael had gone. I had likely seen their girlish eyes for the last time. I was alone.

As I made my way back to the car to return to the city, the words kept coming back to me, "And the people said?" The answer -- always the same -- echoed across the years, "Amen! Amen! Amen!"

I rolled down the window and breathed deeply of the clean, fresh air, and of freedom. I had answered the call to the 'Homecoming', but I had not come home.

The Best Christmas

"No, Moira. That's not right! Start again at 'Go to the ant'..." But it was of no use. The small, nine-year old girl in the tattered dress stumbled over the words and nineteen-year old Amy Wagner was at her wits' end. "I don't know what will become of you!" she said, looking sorrowfully at the child.

Matt didn't know either. Moira seemed alright at home when she wasn't doing school work. But doing school work she just seemed dumb. Sometimes he thought she tried to be that way. She was becoming an increasing embarrassment. Maybe she'd even be put back a grade. He dropped his gaze to his desk. Then, in a quick turn of his head he scolded her with his eyes.

The big box stove belted out its usual friendly sounds and the large kettle on its top steam-sang its message that the jars of homemade soup were ready. The pretty, black-haired teacher glanced out the window to the snowy north road and the forty children of her one-room school watched her carefully for any sign of the little smile. That smile would tell them there'd be a practice for their Christmas Concert, that is, if Mrs. Ralston could come to play the old church organ for them. Finally they thought they could see the little smile, but it seemed to have some doubt in it. They held their breaths, quiet as mice as she decided.

"Boys," she said to Matt and Tommy, "take this note to Mrs. Eastwood. You can leave when you've finished your sandwiches."

"We'll eat them on the way," Matt said. And with that they were out the door and running down the road to Mrs. Eastwood's place a mile away. The painful tingling in their hands from the hard strapping for swearing was gone, now there was a different kind of tingling spreading right through them because of the importance of their mission.

"You know what?" Tommy said.

"What?" Matt questioned.

"I bet Mrs. Eastwood gives us somethin' to eat for bringin' the note. She did the last time!"

"Let's hurry so we can eat and get back before the bell," Matt suggested.

The new, deep snow came over the tops of their low rubber boots as they ploughed down the trackless road. The wet around the tops didn't matter, nothing mattered except getting the note to Mrs. Eastwood.

"You and me is the luckiest ones in the school, you know that?" Tommy said.

"Yeah, but maybe not if Old Man Eastwood is there," Matt remarked. "I'm scared of him!"

Mrs. Eastwood had seen them coming and was at the door. "Come in boys. You sit right down here and have some chocolate cake and maple syrup. I'll see what this note says." She glanced at the note, then quickly went out to the kitchen to telephone.

"See, I told you!" Tommy said.

"Yeah, and the old man isn't here to see us gettin' his syrup either!" Matt whispered, giggling.

"I'll bet Mrs. Ralston's getting that old nag hooked to the cutter right now!" Mrs. Eastwood stated, handing them a note for the teacher, winking reassuredly.

The boys raced back through the heavy snow and ran into the school breathless just as the bell stopped ringing.

"She's comin', Miss Wagner, she's comin'!" Matt called out, handing her the note.

"And she's gonna bring the cutter, too, with the sleigh bells!" Tommy added, spreading the excitement.

"Children!" the teacher called, sharply. She spoke to them that way quite often, and they could tell from her voice when she was angry and when she wasn't. And they knew she wasn't angry this time. And they knew that she was as excited about the concert as they were, but they didn't let on that they knew. They all got quietly down to work.

As three o'clock approached they strained their ears to catch any sound of the tinkling, crystal sleigh bells on Mrs. Ralston's cutter. Then they heard them -- coming like music, right across the clear blue of the sky. The few moments they listened seemed like forever as they sat on the edge of their seats waiting for the signal to move.

"Alright," she said, and they burst from their seats and bounded across the road to the church. They had just sat down when the back door opened, and Mrs. Ralston peeked her head around the corner. Her little nose was all red from the cold and her funny-looking, gold-rimmed glasses were all steamed over. She put them on the table, then took off her big, red scarf and the heavy, home-knit hat.

"It's lovely to be with you," she said, with the same warm smile she always had for them. They all knew that she liked them, and they thought it might be because she didn't have any children of her own. She went straight to the old pump organ and stretched her short, plump legs down to reach the pedals.

"Fetch my glasses, please Moira," she said. "I want to see my children, you know!"

"They're like my grandma's!" Moira said excitedly. "She came to stay with us for Christmas."

"You're a granny!" Mrs. Ralston joked, slipping her glasses on the small girl, bringing giggles from the children. And even the teacher giggled.

"Nobody touches my grandma's glasses!" Moira said, with a note of caution.

Mrs. Ralston's fingers came down on the keys and the Colonel Bogey march sprang out of the old organ. Nobody could make the marches roll out like she could. What fun it was to do the drills with her playing. And the songs after -- the ones the singing teacher who came every two weeks had taught them.

Mrs. Brenton wouldn't be coming any more though. There was no money to pay her, the trustees said. Everybody was sorry about it except Mrs. Cordy. She said it was 'wasted money' teaching kids to sing -- they could do that by themselves.

"You sound just lovely!" Mrs. Ralston said, when they had finished the practice. "And to sing harmony so well. Mrs. Brenton has done splendidly with you." Her warm eyes moved along the three rows of children, hesitating for a moment on each child.

"One more practice and we'll have this polished up like your noses on concert night!" she said, laughing with them. "Well, I had better jingle-bell my horse along home before it gets dark." When she reached the door she turned and called back to them, "I guess I'll have to sing all by myself on the way home. My horse has a voice like a train whistle with a bad cold!" She paused outside the door for a moment. She could still hear their laughter. "Lovely children," she said out loud to herself. "And they're mine...for a little while."

The next day Moira's homework was all correct and the teacher became suspicious.

"Oh please, it's a secret!" the excited girl tried to explain.

"A secret?" the teacher questioned, looking straight at the girl.

"Oh please," Moira said, cowering and squinting up at the teacher. "It's a secret about my grandma's glasses."

Amy Wagner looked into the deep blue eyes of the girl. "How could I have been so unimaginative -- so careless?" she questioned, now visibly distraught.

"Oh, Miss Wagner, are you sick?" Moira asked innocently.

"I'm sure everything will be alright now, Moira," the teacher replied quietly.

On concert night Matt and Moira hurried along the road to the church with their mother and older sister Stephanie. Matt talked excitedly to Moira, striding along, sniffing in great breaths of frosty air, freezing his nostrils together momentarily. He felt a special joy tugging at his heart this night. From the way she talked, he thought his mother felt the way he did. He was glad for her, because there had not been much for her to be joyful about since the summer. Even the jack rabbits seemed happy as they bounded over the snow amongst the corn shocks standing like small fortresses in the moonlight. Underneath some of those shocks of corn Matt knew there would be warm, fat mice. Even that seemed to be the way it should be on this night. Above them the northern lights, making strange music, danced in wispy twirls across the face of the moon of wintertime. It was as though all nature was in tune with the wondrous night. Matt forgot all about the pinching shoes he borrowed from his cousin in town.

Inside the church the naptha gas lights were burning. The smell of spruce boughs mingled with the smell of popcorn balls, perfume, home made candy, new broadcloth of boys' shirts, wax crayons and the paper around the presents.

24

The children were all in the front rows, ready to mount the platform at the signal. Some of them thought they would burst if that chairman didn't hurry up. While they waited they could see Ole looking over at the teacher quite a lot. They thought they caught her throwing a couple of smiles in his direction when nobody was looking. They put their heads down and snickered a little and passed smiles along to each other with their eyes. They thought she liked Ole, because she wouldn't go with him in his car if she didn't like him. But maybe it was because he was the only young man who had a car. They didn't know.

Now it was their turn. Quickly they stepped up to the platform to do all the things they had been practising so hard for. The people clapped their hands after every number. Some of the people's faces started getting red from the warmth in the crowded church. Some parents were nodding their heads in agreement with other parents sitting beside them. And Old Man Eastwood was smiling. He was never like that any other time. Men and women who would hardly speak to each other most of the time, were sitting by each other having a good time and laughing with each other. The children looked down at them. They knew it was all happening because of what they were doing up there on the stage. And they were glad about that.

Then it was over. They packed up their gifts and the popcorn balls Mrs. Eastwood had brought and started for home.

"You know what I heard?" Tommy said to Matt when they were outside.

"What?"

"Old maid Jensen said she was gonna give the money to keep the singin' teacher!"

"You better not call her that if she's gonna give the money." Matt cautioned.

"Alright, I won't. And it's a secret, too. Nobody knows."

"I won't tell," Matt promised.

The children straggled along behind the parents, talking and singing on the way home. Matt took off the tight shoes to let his feet feel the fresh cold of the dry, frozen grass at the edge of the road. When they came to the mailbox where the parents were waiting they stopped singing. They could hear Matt's mother saying, "I wish he could have heard them sing. It will be the first Christmas without him."

"Keep singing your part as you go down the road, we'll do the harmony," Stephanie called to the neighbouring children. 'Away in a Manger' rang out across the winter fields at midnight.

Moira was watching Mrs. Eastwood throw popcorn balls at Mr. Eastwood for saying there would be no more concerts, when Stephanie pulled the covers from over her head the next morning and shook her out of her dream.

"We'll have to hurry," Stephanie said, her voice sounding far away. "We don't want to be late for the clean-up."

Ole was just letting the teacher out of his car when they reached the church. He was moving a lot faster than he usually did when he opened the car door for her. His face didn't go all red when he saw them, like it did before. He looked a lot stronger too and he smiled at them like he really meant it.

The teacher brought the small victrola from the school so they could listen to Christmas carols while they worked and in no time they had the church cleaned. Nothing was left of the concert decorations but the Christmas tree. Then it was back to the school for the hot chocolate they had been promised. Maybe, they thought, the teacher would have a small gift for each of them.

"Come up to the front, children," she said. She pulled a large box from under her desk and drew from it sets of water colours with their names all spelled in fancy writing. Then she lifted the map covering the black board. There, in her fine art work were the words Merry Christmas in large, white letters like the ones on the Books of Knowledge. There were two cherubs, a boy and a girl, out at the ends holding up the words. And around the edges were green leaves of mistletoe and red berries.

"It's my Christmas Card for you," she exclaimed.

"I bet it's the best Christmas Card in the whole world!" Tommy said proudly. Matt looked long and hard at the card the teacher had designed just for them. "Yeah, it is." he said.

When the teacher let them go, she asked Moira to stay behind. She put her arm around the small girl's shoulder and gave her a gentle hug, just as Ole came through the door.

"Take this envelope to your mother," she said. She looked for a moment into the wide, questioning eyes of the girl. "Those eyes are going to discover lots of wonderful secrets soon," she said.

"Oh, Miss Wagner," Moira burst out, "isn't this the best Christmas there could ever be?"

Amy Wagner glanced at Ole, then down at the sparkling diamond. "Yes Moira, that's right. That's right!" she said.

The Firemakers

Coe Anderson and Eve McCarthy walked briskly through the high courthouse doors and started down the long row of steps.

"I'll take that," Coe said, reaching for Eve's briefcase. It felt good to have it close to him, for that briefcase contained the verification that he had survived the terrible twelve years. A few steps down, he stopped and let the events of those years, so far as he could remember them, race through his brain one more time. Maybe most of them would not have occurred if he hadn't taken that slab of hard maple for the back of the violin he was making. Maybe then they would have believed he was telling the truth about the house fire.

Nobody else would want the dirty, ancient-looking violin brought down from Old Man Robinson's attic for the auction sale, Coe thought. Then he saw a big stranger squinting through one of the sound holes at the tattered paper tag stuck to its back.

"Could be a Stradivarius," he said in a subdued voice to the well-dressed woman beside him.

"Five dollars...going...Sold!" the auctioneer shouted from his wagon-box platform. Coe put the thirty-five cents back in his pocket and headed for home.

The cold stung his wet feet with every step as he plodded across the fields through the slushy, March snow. He couldn't get his mind off the violin. He thought it might sound just like the one he heard the day

Mrs. Macmillan brought her radio to school. She wanted them all to hear some special music by a great conductor broadcasting from New York. He knew now he'd have to make his own violin if he was ever going to have one. Every cent his mother could get her hands on went for the simple necessities of life, and the insurance.

'Keep up the insurance,' his dad had cautioned his mother, as he lay dying from the war wound. She promised she would, and she did, by picking berries, and scrubbing floors for some of the better-off women of Buttonwood. Coe knew she worked too hard, but she wouldn't let him quit school to help her. 'Learning is the key for an imprisoned mind,' she'd say.

After a week in the hospital in London his mother was no better, Dr. Morrison told him, and he seemed sad when he said it. That same night after dark Sandy Downs came to the door and asked him if he'd help snitch a few blocks from Broadbent's big woodpile down on the corner lot. Sandy said he knew it was wrong, but his family were all sick in bed and there was no wood for a fire to get the dampness out of the house. The poor Irish family consisting of a mother and three children had drifted into the community and moved into a derelict house by the railroad tracks at the edge of town. Sandy, seventeen like himself, acted real strange sometimes. He even got violently angry a few times when they were walking home from school. When that happened he'd invite Sandy into the house and his mother would always give them something to eat. 'That boy is suffering from malnutrition,' she'd say. 'It's some decent food he needs, and a warm place to stay.' After hearing his mother say that, it seemed alright now to help Sandy grab a few blocks of Broadbent's wood.

They quietly skirted the high board fence on the dark side of the lot and crept along a row of shrubs, keeping out of the light. They quickly filled two sacks and hurried back along the board fence.

"Stop right where you are! Stop, you young hellions! You're up to something!" The raspy voice froze them in their steps for an instant. Then they raced away into the darkness.

"It's Bardsley, the insurance man," Sandy whispered, when they were out of danger. "I don't think he could tell it was us."

At Sandy's house they took the wood from the sacs and soon a good fire was sending cheer into the old house. Mrs. Downs came from her dark bedroom and said she thought she might be feeling better. She'd make some tea on the hot stove, she said, but they'd have to drink it without milk. As Coe was leaving for home he picked up a thin slab of hard maple.

"I can make a back for my fiddle out of this," he stated.

"I'm worried about your mother, Coe," Dr. Morrison said, when he came back from the hospital the next day. "I wish I had something else I could tell you, son." That night Coe let his dog, Luke, into the house because a storm was brewing. Then he went upstairs to his room to work on his violin. It would help him to keep his mind off his mother he thought. He looked closely at the sketches he made at the library and began to whittle the hard maple slab for the back. The wood was extremely hard to work, but it would all be worthwhile, he told himself, when it became part of the instrument he had so painstakingly crafted thus far.

When searching the library index for 'Instruments', he had run across the word 'Inquisition', and he read all that was written about it in the encyclopedia. When the word came up in history class, he noticed Eve's interest pick up. She had more sense than the other girls, he thought. And she liked him some, even if she did live on the good side of town and her father was the magistrate. She squeezed his hand a little the night she broke her leg at the outdoor skating rink and he carried her all the way to Dr. Morrison's office without stopping. It felt good to hold her, even if he was just carrying her. Now, as he carefully shaped the pieces of the violin, his thoughts slipped back to his mother in the hospital. He began to visualize the doctors conducting an Inquisition in her room, ruling on whether or not she would live. He began to work furiously carving the hard maple, but the thoughts of his mother and the Inquisition would not leave him. He thought of the millions of people, mostly women, tied to stakes and burned. His mother would have been one of them because of her outspokenness. And Sandy's too and....

"Luke!" he cried in a breaking voice. The dog bounded up the stairs to his side.

"What are we going to do?" he implored, putting his arms around the dog. Finally he was able to compose himself, and he sent the dog downstairs to his place by the stove. He turned out the light and got into bed. Soon he was asleep.

A violent crashing sound shook Coe into semi-consciousness. Then the dog landed heavily on his bed, pawing at the covers until he was fully awake. The bedroom was filled with smoke and flames were licking up the staircase.

"Wake up mother!" he yelled to the dog, forgetting that she was in the hospital. He spun around to get his violin, but the place where he left it was engulfed in flames. He hesitated a moment, then dove for the window gasping for air. As his brain cleared he crawled through the window and dropped to the ground. The house now resembled a flaming chimney, and soon it was burned to the ground.

"It could have been lightning," the volunteer firechief said when they got there too late. But no one remembered seeing any lightning, although some living nearby thought they heard thunder roll across the sky. They remained skeptical, for they all agreed that thunder in March was virtually unknown in the area. One old man in the country declared that he saw a fireball fly over his barn in the direction of Buttonwood, but no one paid any attention to the man who was thought to be slightly senile.

Felix Bardsley knew that Coe had gone to Sandy's house for the night. Early the next morning he rapped heavily on Sandy's door. There'd have to be an investigation, he said, and likely the head office would send a man down because of the strange circumstances surrounding the fire.

"Funny thing that a fire would start in a heavy rain, I'd think," Bardsley said, looking suspiciously at Coe. Sandy began to get nervous and started to put some wood on the fire.

"Good looking wood," Bardsley commented, "Same quality I buy from Broadbents." Then he was gone, and the boys began to worry that Bourdon, the policeman, would soon show up.

"I saw spirits hiding in the woodpile the night we snitched the wood!" Sandy stated suddenly the next day, just as Bourdon got back into his car. "And there are bad spirits down at Bridge Creek under the railroad. I can't take the short-cut down the track any more. I told the Father about it, and he said not to go that way. I told him what you said about the millions burned in the Inquisition. He said it was the bad people who wouldn't believe, who caused the trouble. They wouldn't believe in the Faith. You know something? He said I shouldn't listen to you about such things."

"There are no spirits down at the railroad bridge in the spring floods, Sandy. That's superstition. They just say that to scare the little kids away from the high water. And there are no spirits in the woodpile, either!"

"The way to get rid of bad spirits is to burn them!" Sandy blurted out, his eyes now fierce with determination. "That's how the Inquisition did it." That night Broadbent's woodpile went up in flames.

"Eve, I think I know you pretty well," Dr. Morrison said, when he called her from across the street. "I'm going down now to tell the Anderson boy of his mother's death. It might make a difference if you came along. He seems to hardly have a friend left after the rumours about the fire."

"Give me a minute to comb my hair," Eve said, "and I'll be ready."

"Rumours can be mighty cruel sometimes," the doctor remarked, as they drove along slowly. "Making that boy a target at a time like this. Maybe I shouldn't be spending my life trying to help such people."

"I know he's innocent." Eve stated adamantly. "He just wouldn't do the things they're accusing him of doing!"

"Your dad seemed a bit upset when I asked about bringing you along."

"It's because of his job," she explained. "He's under immense pressure from some of the influential people in town. Even the priest and Reverend Nilshott have gotten in on it. And Reverend Nilshott saying 'the boy is headed for the fires of hell' the way he's going now. Perhaps he and the priest could 'do something to change the wayward nature of the boy'. Exorcism is what they mean! And this before he has even been charged with anything."

"I didn't know you felt so strongly, my girl," the doctor said. "I'm rather glad I asked you to come along!"

Coe and Sandy were chopping wood when the car drove up in front of the Downs' house.

"She's gone...I know that's what you're here to tell me." Coe said, dropping the axe to the ground.

"I'm sorry son," the doctor said, putting a comforting hand on the boy's shoulder. "Eve is going to stay for a little. I'll pick her up when I've finished the country flu cases. You come and see me any time you like."

On the morning of the inquiry into the house fire, Sandy insisted on going with Coe. He'd have to wait outside, but he'd be there if Coe needed him.

"Coe Anderson," Magistrate Alvin McCarthy began, "You've been summoned here, as I'm sure you are aware, to answer some questions concerning the fire at the residence of your late mother.... We all extend our sympathy on the loss of your mother. The only charge filed against you at this time is one of misdemeanour, resulting from your having taken some wood from Broadbent's corner lot. But it is the house we are here to deal with and this inquiry is designed to determine if there is sufficient evidence to warrant charges. Only those parties having a direct interest in the matter of the fire and their counsels, are permitted to attend this hearing. Now, before we begin, have you any questions?"

"No, Sir."

"Place your hand on the bible and swear to tell the truth."

"I cannot do that," Coe replied.

"But it is the law," Magistrate McCarthy informed him.

"I cannot do it," Coe repeated.

"Don't you believe in the bible?" Felix Bardsley butted in.

"No."

"I'll handle this," the magistrate stated, turning to Bardsley. "You'll get your turn."

"Mr. Anderson," Alvin McCarthy cautioned, "You must cooperate."

"I promise to tell the truth," Coe replied.

"We'll proceed," Magistrate McCarthy stated. "You may begin your questioning, Mr. Aspen."

Jonathan Aspen, special investigator for the Latchford Insurance Company, turned slowly and fixed his cold, glaring eyes on the boy.

"We have established beyond doubt that the fire was started from inside your mother's residence, with the aid of some flammable substance of an undetermined nature. You were the only one in the house that night. Is that not true?"

"Luke was with me."

"Luke?" the investigator queried.

"My dog, Luke."

"I suppose Luke set the fire!" Bardsley burst in, raising a laugh from all but the magistrate. "By the way, where is the dog?"

"I sent him to wake mother, and he never came back," Coe explained.

"But your mother was in the hospital," Bardsley countered.

"I was only half awake. I forgot," the boy stated.

"It's obvious this boy is playing with us," Constable Bourdon interjected, sarcastically.

"What were you doing the night of the fire?" Bardsley demanded.

"I was working on my violin," Coe replied. "I was making a violin."

"And how does a boy your age go about making a violin?" Bardlsey asked, superciliously.

"It takes plans, good seasoned wood and lots of careful work."

35

"What kind of wood?" Bardsley pressed.

"Pine and maple."

"There'd be lots of shavings to start a fire," Bardsley said, accusingly. "By the way, where did you get the hard maple?" Coe didn't answer immediately, worried that he might implicate Sandy. But when Magistrate McCarthy raised his eyes in serious expectation, he knew he must answer.

"From Broadbents," he said quietly.

Bardsley leaned back in his chair with a satisfied smile, and nodded to Bourdon.

"Broadbents. And later you burned the woodpile to destroy the evidence. And scattered the ashes to cover your footprints."

"I didn't burn the woodpile!" Coe stated, emphatically.

"You're lying!" Bardsley shouted. "You're lying about everything. You should be in jail!"

"Mr. Bardsley!" Magistrate McCarthy called, his stern eyes reaching over the rims of his glasses, "This is an inquiry -- not an inquisition. It will be up to Mr. Bourdon to lay criminal charges if he feels it necessary."

"There'll be no insurance paid out," Bardsley stated, adamantly. "This boy is lying. He has a bad streak in him! He burned the old house to get the insurance money when his poor mother was dying in the hospital. And he burned Broadbent's woodpile!"

Just as Magistrate McCarthy was about to demand the withdrawal of Bardsley's accusations the door flew open and Sandy Downs burst into the room, saliva frothing from his lips, his face chalk white under his flaming red hair.

"I burned the woodpile. I burned the damn thing to kill the bad spirits. I burned it! I burned it! I burned the spirits!" And with that he collapsed, falling face down on the floor. The group sat in shocked silence for a moment.

Then McCarthy hastened Bourdon forward, jumping to his feet at the same time.

"This boy is terribly sick. Check to see if the doctor has left for the city," he ordered, turning the boy over to ensure his breathing.

"He's starving," Coe said quietly.

"What do you mean?" Bardsley demanded.

"He's starving," Coe repeated. "His whole family is starving."

"This hearing stands adjourned," the magistrate said firmly. "It's obvious to me that we won't be able to continue until this boy is completely recovered and able to give testimony."

"That boy has to be sent away," Bardsley persisted, as he followed McCarthy into his office early the next morning. "He's a pyromaniac, a real danger to the community. Even the Father and Reverend Nilshott say that."

"But we are not sure he is guilty of anything but taking a slab of wood!" McCarthy protested.

"Now look Alvin, if we let this boy off and he gets into more trouble, how is it going to look for you and your chance to get the nod for the bench? You hinted yourself that you don't want to jeopardize Eve's chances for the law scholarship. She's at that impressionable age right now. That young hellion has a bad streak I tell you...he doesn't even believe in the bible! And there's something else. The Company is thinking of putting a Regional Office here in a couple of years. If that Anderson property comes up for tax default, it will be a perfect site. The Company would pay a good dollar for that land. Think what a Regional Office would mean for all of us." Alvin McCarthy put his head down and closed his eyes for a few seconds. Bardsley sat watching him, his clamped jaws rippling his cheek muscles. When

McCarthy opened his eyes Bardlsey spit out some news he had been holding back.

"Bourdon and I talked late into the night. We agreed on what we think should be done. He's making out a charge of arson this very minute."

"That pretty well takes it out of my hands," McCarthy said, a tone of resignation plainly discernible in his words. "I'll recommend to Judge Armand that he be sent to a Correctional Institution if he's found guilty. I wouldn't like to see the boy go into the Federal System. It would be safer to have it over with before he turns eighteen." He reached for his phone.

"Old Judge Armand knows how to deal with guys like him!" Bardsley remarked, stepping quickly from the office.

Eve's friend, Amy, was at the railway station the day they took Coe away. She told him that Eve had become hysterical and struck out at her father the night before when she learned of the two-year sentence. They called Dr. Morrison and he put her in the Red Cross Hospital overnight.

Coe had been in the Correctional Institution only two weeks when word came that Sandy Downs had run headlong into an express train screaming that the bad spirits could never get him again. Coe wept in his loneliness the day the news came, but he made sure no one saw him, because the institution was no place to show weakness. He put most of his time into his studies, for his mother's words, 'Education is the key for an imprisoned mind' were never far away from him. How little she could have known that her words would one day have double meaning. His studies became the one reality he clung to. Still, he worried about his sanity sometimes, especially when he'd wake up in a sweat after dreaming of the Inquisition fires licking up around his dog tied to the stake. He wondered why Eve didn't write to him, even though he knew from Amy's first letter that Eve's father had forbidden her to write. The Institution post mark would draw immediate attention at the post office, he said. In one letter Amy told him that Eve had taken a part-time job with the town clerk. The experience would help her when she studied law.

The two years passed surprisingly quickly for Coe. In another two weeks he would be free. But the elation generated by the thought of freedom was now having to compete with his worry about the increasing restlessness of the inmates. The prolonged heat wave could easily touch off trouble. Only a few days to go now, Coe thought, as he marched with the others into the stifling heat of the mess hall for the evening meal. No one seemed to notice that the placement had put two sworn enemies across the table from each other.

"Garbage!" one man shouted, aiming his plate of food directly at his adversary. The fight spread with a suddenness and a violence that took the guards by surprise. In a few seconds most of the inmates were caught up in kicking, biting, choking and stabbing, in an animal madness that ripped away the feeble constraints of inmate discipline to free the killer instinct in trapped men. Then the mess hall was ablaze fed by cans of cooking oil. When it was over two men lay dead in the blackened shell. Others who had been stabbed and some who had been pounded until their faces were masses of red pulp, left their blood streaking the hallways as the guards hurried them to the hospital. The rest were herded into a holding yard.

Coe escaped serious injury, but he had not escaped completely, for in a search of the cells his gymnasium bag was found to contain a lighter and two handfuls of lint from the clothes dryer. Such evidence, coupled with the testimony of three inmates who swore they saw him help set the fire, was enough to get him two more years. It could only be Fat Fabro, the guard, who planted the lighter and lint in his bag. Coe was certain of that. The realization of the severity of the additional sentence slowly drew Coe into a depression. Thoughts of suicide now struggled in fierce competition with the thought that Eve might still care for him. He had not heard anything about her for several months after Amy found a boy friend and wasn't interested in writing any more.

"Here," Fat Fabro growled, throwing a letter through the bars. "Why anybody at the law school would want anything to do with you, I can't figure. Maybe you got next to some of them damn do-gooders that make it tough for us guys."

"Thanks," Coe said politely, as he picked up the official-looking brown envelope. When Fabro was out of sight he quickly ripped open the letter.

"I thought it best to use this disguise," Eve began. "There's less likelihood of censorship." She still believed in his innocence, she said, and she would write when she had time. She was very busy studying law. She was sure he'd understand that. But what if she did forget him and found a young man at law school she liked, Coe asked himself.

Her letters came at intervals of about three months, always containing something encouraging, always tempered by a conservative choice of words. He thought of her each night as he tried to get to sleep. Sometimes she got mixed up in his strange dreams about his dog, his mother, the Inquisition and Sandy Downs. Sometimes Eve was one of the women marked for burning at the stake. And sometimes he could see the priest and Reverend Nilshott laughing and shaking hands as the flames curled around Eve. When he woke up screaming, the other inmates would yell, "Shut up, you crazy bastard!" Maybe he was crazy, he thought. But if he saw a doctor that would be a sign of weakness. If he could just hang on until his sentence was finished. He'd be only twenty-two -- still young. He might even go to law school.

"Get your things together, Anderson," Fat Fabro ordered, sneering through the bars. "You're on parole. You're not going to be a damn bit happier about this than I am!"

Coe quickly mustered his discipline and resisted any response.

"They've got a job for you too, in a big city packing house. Just right for a blood and guts guy like you!" Fabro turned away, laughing at his own humour. "You've got fifteen minutes. It'd be a shame if you weren't ready, wouldn't it?" he said threateningly, rattling his stick noisily across the bars.

"It's the bacon table in the morning and the kill floor in the afternoon," the foreman said, in an east-European accent. "Got to keep killing them, or there's no bacon to trim."

It seemed simple enough work, slicing the lean, red slivers from strips of fat trimmed from bacon sides. But soon Coe's right hand began to swell from the constant pushing of the knife through cold, hard fat, and he was falling behind.

"I'll help you a little until you get broken in," the small man called to him across the wide table. "Then you'll be alright. When I came from the old country after the war, my violin-playing hands objected, just like yours." The man's face reflected a sincere smile and Coe felt a sudden surge of confidence and renewal of hope. It was as though the world was finally opening to him. He was moving out into the sunshine and the warmth of that sunshine was racing to every tissue of his being. He was coming alive again. He was walking into life. Real life! The way it used to be. And in a short while he might see Eve!

41

"Thanks," he said, almost too enthusiastically. "I'll try to get onto it as fast as I can." The small man smiled again and dropped his eyes to the cold sides of bacon.

"Your job is to help shackle the pigs," the kill-floor foreman shouted over the noise. "It looks hard, but you'll pick it up fast. Just slip the shackle on one hind leg. The hoist does the rest. You have to be quick. Watch how it's done for a while, then try it."

The first few tries were failures. Several times Coe found himself on his hands and knees amongst the milling pigs' feet. Then he hooked one, and the squealing pig was jerked off its feet and hoisted up to the kill floor. There the skilled sticker was ready with his sharp knife. One quick plunge and a twist of the knife was all that was required to send the hot blood pouring through the small incision and the struggling pig was soon lifeless. Suddenly Coe was conscious of the stench of hot blood and steam as pigs slid into the scalding tank. He almost vomited, but the shackler's promise of relief in a few minutes caused him to bite his lip and keep going. Finally relief came.

"You can go up and help the sticker," the shackler said. "Keep his knives sharp or something. I'll do the couple hundred left." Coe climbed the steel stairs to the sticker's platform. He watched horrified, yet fascinated, as the skilled sticker did his grizzly job time after time. The sticker turned and smiled once. He couldn't tell whether it was a friendly smile, or just a smile of satisfaction with his skill.

"Would you like to try it?" the sticker asked, blood pouring down his leather-sheathed arm. "It's easy when you know how to find the jugular." Coe quickly stepped back, shaking his head. "I'll sharpen your knives if you wish," he offered.

"I've got a half dozen. There's no need."

Coe's nights became nights of terror, with dreams of the killing floor on which pigs sometimes became people. When his screams brought threats of eviction from the landlady he resorted to strong sleeping pills, but they were of little use. He could feel himself slipping into a world where fantasy and reality were becoming inseparable. Some of the men were refusing to work with him.

"What's wrong?" the sticker asked one afternoon when he noticed the strange look on Coe's face. "You look angry. Did I say something I shouldn't have?" Coe did not answer. "My God, man, you look terrible! You'd better go downstairs and see the nurse." Coe struck out at the sticker, knocking the knife from his hand.

"Stop! Stop the killing! Stop the Inquisition!" he yelled, and collapsed against the bloody rail.

"I think he's gone crazy," the sticker blurted to the foreman who was watching. "There's something damn wrong with that man. Lucky he didn't grab a knife and come at me!"

Most of the last eight years were a blank, Coe now realized, as he looked in the mirror while he struggled awkwardly with the toothbrush. 'Time has a way of achieving unexpected results' the doctor had remarked the day before. Time...a lot of it gone forever, he thought, as he noticed how much he had aged. Still, time had been on his side, for time had made him well again.

"So Bardsley's Insurance Company came close to getting my property. And that for a dollar!"

"They were a bit too anxious, it seems," Eve remarked. "When my dad saw the excavating equipment working that morning on the way to his office, a strange feeling came over him, he said. They were tearing up the place which had been his boyhood playground. For some

43

reason he decided to check to see if the three-year grace period for taxes had expired. There was one day left, because the last day fell on a statutory holiday. He quickly had the bank call the clerk's office. After that it was a simple matter of a few dollars each year for the taxes."

"But if they hadn't started digging, that geology student on a summer construction job wouldn't have found the forty-pound meteorite buried twelve feet below the house site."

"The 'Anderson Meteorite'," Eve said, with notable satisfaction. "That's what the professor called it when Judge Armand asked him to identify the little piece of charred wood embedded in it."

"The hard maple clinched it. That incredibly small fraction of my violin -- the only thing that survived!"

"I think not," Eve countered. "There's principle, and there's a Mr. Anderson, I believe." Coe closed his eyes and nodded his head in affirmation.

"And the place is still mine. And the insurance -- with interest! Judge Armand was adamant about that." He turned quickly to Eve.

"Do you think a fellow coming thirty-one is too old to...start something?"

"You're not thinking of...?"

"A fire?" he said, laughing. "Not that kind."

"Well," Eve responded, "If I may counter with a question. Do you think a twenty-nine year old lawyer, once divorced, would be a fit candidate to help you...start something?"

"Come on," he said, taking her hand firmly in his. "What's that about phoenix...and ashes?"

Trapped

The sun was a fierce, blazing ball resting on the western horizon when Elmo Crennie propped his hoe against the post at the end of the tobacco row. He had finished his last day's work. Tomorrow the place would belong to somebody else. He threw off his hat and mopped back his shaggy grey hair. He leaned against the post and reached into his pocket for the dried tobacco leaf in the small can. He was hardly conscious of grinding it with his thumb in the cup of his hand and rolling it in the piece of brown paper, then sticking it with his saliva. It was tomorrow that was on his mind. He looked up to watch the buzzards corkscrew their way down the hot air column to the top of the tulip tree, as they always did at that time of day. That was something you could always count on -- the buzzards. He drew the strong smoke past his dirty teeth and deep into his lungs.

Darkness surrounded the small cabin as he ambled up to the door. He lowered his wasted body into the same sweaty bunk where he had slept forty years, ever since he built the cabin on the edge of the bush where he had taken up squatter's rights. He had planned on building a bigger house closer to the road, but when Caroline left him he forgot about it.

Not once had he spent a night away from the cabin, except the time he got caught in a storm while stalking a deer. He stumbled onto a hollow log just as the blackness of the bush locked him to the spot. Not once had he been to the city forty miles to the east people talked about. He rode his horse to Buttonwood, a few miles away, once before winter, once in the spring to get the tea, salt and flour he needed to go with the honey and meat from the bush. For several years he had struggled to coax his living from the poor soil. When the tobacco came in he grabbed at the chance to grow a few acres, doing all the work himself.

The summer heat in the cabin was oppressive. He listened to the night sounds and thought back on the years spent in the bush and swamp, alone and forsaken by all but a cow and a calf or two, three horses and a dog. This would be his last night in the swamp, he told himself. Tomorrow he'd have the money and he'd leave this damned place forever and go find Caroline. The lawyer had told him he'd get the land money soon, along with his pension, when he had gotten Crennie to put his X on the piece of paper, signing the place over to the new people. The money from the land would take care of him and Caroline when he found her.

The misery he felt at this time each night was softening as he grew sleepy. He thought about how he had crowded the bush and swamp a little more each year, how he had gained a few acres with nobody being the wiser and about how he turned in the fugitive, Brome, who was hiding out in the bush during the bad times. The reward had helped him to get started in the tobacco. And there was the murder in the swamp which he hadn't said anything about because any investigation might have shown that he had taken land which wasn't his.

He dropped off to sleep, but in a few seconds he awoke with a start. He felt afraid. It wasn't normal for him to be afraid in the night. He puzzled over it until exhaustion again took him into sleep. After a few minutes he awoke for the second time. It was strange, he thought, that on this last night in the cabin he couldn't stay asleep. It must be the screaming bobcats in the deep bush, he told himself. But the old dog lying beside the bunk wasn't anxious, so everything must be alright, he reasoned. He raised himself up on his elbow as his wracking cough began to tear at his chest once more. After a while the burning eased and he stretched out again. He lifted one leg out and felt the dog pressed tightly against the bottom boards. It gave him a feeling of security. But the coughing spell had shaken him badly. The spells had been getting worse and this last year he'd been much less able to work. Maybe he should stop the tobacco like the mailman said. He'd think about it in the morning. He was too tired to decide now.

After a few minutes he found himself in a kind of dream state. He thought it was just another one of the times that often came to him after the coughing spells, when he couldn't seem to get enough air to keep his thinking straight and he'd see things which weren't there. He found himself in a large, strange room made of vines and branches, closed on all sides. Animals, birds and trees were positioned in a circle around him with a large, ferocious-looking beaver holding the most prominent position. The beaver quickly scanned the gathering, then turned to Crennie,

"Your name!" he demanded, baring his sharp teeth. There was no answer.

"Your Name!" he again demanded, his fierce, black eyes now fixed on the prisoner in a contemptuous stare. Crennie found himself paralyzed, unable to talk, unable to move. No matter how desperately he struggled, he could bring no answer to his lips for the beaver judge. The beaver slapped his large tail smartly on the log bench. His long whiskers oscillated in an intimidating manner.

"Your real name!" he roared. When there was still no reply, the judge declared that the charges would be heard. The lynx was the first to approach the bench.

"Honourable rodent, I charge this species with killing my grandfather."

"He took my new-born calf in broad daylight!" the prisoner found himself saying. "He came right into the

47

yard and dragged the little calf away into the bush. After he had his fill, he fell asleep and I found him. I put a bullet through the bastard's head. That was the end of him! I had to give what was left of the calf to the buzzards!" Crennie recalled the day when he had faced a lynx for the first time. He had been walking into an east wind when he came upon the lynx behind a mound of old hay, just as the lynx was about to pounce on a sleeping rabbit. They had both frozen for a fraction of a second as their eyes burned into each other's. Then each backed away. Crennie had never forgotten. He had hated and feared the lynx from that day forward. He had hated most of the animals of the bush and swamp. They all made it hard for a man, he said. The only ones that didn't do any harm were the buzzards. They picked up the remains of what the others destroyed. "You fellas is my friends," he'd say sometimes, as he watched the huge, black vultures quietly soaring in wide circles over the bush and swamp.

"Black rat snake," called the judge. "Your charge!" The great snake slid silently across the grassy floor and focussed his glassy eyes on the prisoner, his tongue shooting out menacingly towards the man's throat. He coiled himself up close to the charged man.

"He has killed many of my family over the years, with sticks, guns and axes."

"The slimy bastards took my little chickens from the high ground where they were safe from the rain!" the prisoner blurted out.

"White-tailed deer. Your charge!" barked the judge, showing his anger.

"The garment he is wearing was once the soft skin of a prominent member of our family. The flesh was cut from the bones. The remains were taken by the evil birds!" The buzzards nodded a smiling approval in the man's direction, their ugly, featherless necks and heads bobbing in unison.

"I had no meat and I had no coat for winter," the charged man replied.

"The fluffy tail hanging by the cabin door is from another member of our family. Its throat was ripped out by dogs after a bullet through its lungs dropped it in the swamp."

"Rabbit, what have you got to say?" the judge asked.

"We are victims of many animals," the rabbit replied, as he turned to see the lynx and bobcat passing knowing smiles to each other. The prisoner did not bother to reply. It was obvious that no one attached much importance to rabbits.

The butterfly was next. Perched delicately on a vine, her gentle wings moving slowly and rhythmically, she turned toward the prisoner and explained that the special flowers on which her family depended for their total nectar supply, had been severely depleted when the rough road had been cut through near the swamp. She explained further, that some larval stages were limited to one kind of leaf for food and that because of this her blue cousin had to leave.

Crennie felt a degree of compassion for the colourful, fragile creature and for the first time he began to think that maybe everything in the bush and swamp did belong there.

"There is no time for the badgers, opossums and squirrels," the judge declared. "Trees," he ordered. A noisy chattering caused the judge to reconsider and the squirrels angrily told of their brothers being shot out of trees for sport and sometimes they had been eaten by man.

"Bastards!" the prisoner said under his breath, as he thought of the large female's sharp teeth being sunk into his arm when he had gone too close to her nest of young.

The tulip tree gave a non-too-friendly glance toward the beaver as it recounted how this man had cut one of

49

its aging parents just for the honey in the hollow of its trunk. "In the spring our flowers light the cold sky in soft, delicate reflections, high above the canopy. Later, we and the dogwood send our petals down in a glorious shower to carpet the forest floor."

"Buzzards!" broke in the judge, unable to hide his contempt for the stinking birds. The seven large, greasy, black avions sat with their fierce talons tightly clamped around a branch and spread their six-foot wings in a defiant gesture. The leader opened his mighty, hooked jaws and squawked, "We have no complaints against this animal!" The others lifted and lowered their broad wings sightly three times to show their agreement.

"We'll hear from the golden-winged warbler," advised the judge.

The small bird flew up to a high vine. She lifted her head and expanded her small chest. "I am here alone," she began. "There are very few of us. Indeed, we are known to be rare." She paused for a moment, drawing air deeply into her tiny body. "I survey the land as I soar the blue sky in free flight," she continued, now using all four notes that her voice possessed. "From high above the forests and meadows, the wetlands and the streams, I see the snakes and the frogs, the butterflies and the bees, the flowers and the blossoms, the animals and the birds. When I look down at the beauty of our garden, I often send my song across the domain for all to share my happiness. But sometimes I am sad when I think about the forest and the swamp being reduced, for it means that some of us must go, but some cannot go because we have no place to go. The few remaining members of our families will disappear forever. There will be no delicate throats to send music across the morning skies."

"Have you anything to say, animal?" asked the judge. The charged man struggled to reply, but his jaws were locked.

"You are sentenced," the judge said slowly and deliberately, "to...."

The prisoner made a desperate attempt to break the force binding him. In a convulsive eruption his body was thrown into an upright, sitting position. Suddenly he was awake. A searing pain tore at his chest and every pounding pulse of his frightened heart surged in his lungs in a miniature explosion. He sat on his sweat-soaked bed as water rolled off his forehead in dirty, salty streams, into his eyes and down his neck. For a moment he wasn't sure that he had escaped the dream, but when the old dog licked his left hand still clenching the side of the bunk, he knew he was awake and safe. He put his hand on the dog's head as he had done every morning since he brought it in as a pup, after a huge hawk had taken its mate while its mother held a lynx at bay. He wanted to be especially reassuring to the dog on this last morning, as if to say that everything would be alright.

He pulled on his sweat-stiff shirt and pants, splashed some water on his face from the barrel by the stove, lit the stove, threw a handful of tea into the big tin pot of cold water and placed it on the stove to boil. He pushed open the door and looked out on the rows of green tobacco. Everything would be alright. It had only been a dream. He rolled up some tobacco in a piece of brown paper and ran his wet tongue along the edge to stick it together, then slid the cigarette between his rotten teeth. He stuck the end through a crack in the stove to reach the flames and sucked the smoke deep into his lungs. A fierce pain stabbed at his right lung as the smoke hit it, causing him to put down the cigarette. He thought again about what the mailman had been saying about quitting, but as the pain eased he finished the bitter smoke. He ate dry corn-meal biscuits and drank the tea...he'd be through with the damn corn meal too after this morning! He pulled on his boots for the trip out to the road, then picked up the small, heavy-cloth bag he used for money and headed out the door.

Force of habit made him look up to see if the buzzards were flying, but he knew that it was too early for them. They never got started until the day warmed up. He never figured out why that was. He called them 'lazy buzzards' sometimes. The vultures usually came to his cabin first. They had come to expect something from him. He had always made sure that any animal parts he couldn't use would be left for them.

At the gate, his favorite mare was nuzzling the post. "I can't take you with me, Jess," he said to the mare. "There's no place for horses where I'm goin'." She'd be pulling the boat in the tobacco soon, but it would be for somebody else this time.

He started back along the track, the dream still vivid in his mind. He looked at the place where he had dug out the skunks and clubbed them over their heads before they could spray him. The pelt money from Armstrong's fur auction had bought his spring provisions. The buzzards tore at the pile of carcasses voraciously when they returned in the early spring. He noticed how they went after the eyes first.

He came to the spot in the deep bush where he told the law they could find Brome, the fugitive. The police snapped handcuffs on Brome and chained his legs. He'd never outrun them again, they said. He felt guilty about it now, sending a man to jail for stealing bread and bacon. He himself had stolen when he was hungry. And Brome had brought him venison in the night when he'd been so sick that winter. The reward made the difference. He wouldn't do it again, he thought. He recalled in the dream how the beaver judge was about to pass sentence. It must have been like that for Brome. He tried to forget it.

Gravity pulled hard at his boots with every step and he soon had to stop to rest. He sat down on the stump of the tulip tree he cut for the honey, a few feet away from the spot where he first set eyes on Caroline. The fresh mint tantalized his nose just as it did when she stood there forty years earlier. How pretty she looked, with the warm sun bouncing off the rich, red hair which curled down around her cheeks, framing a milk-white face. Her intensive green eyes had given him a frightened smile as she curtsied. At fifteen she had looked as soft and delicate as the butterflies. At the sight of her a feverish wave rolled over his body sending blood rushing into his neck and face. At that moment he wanted more than anything else in the world to take her in his arms and let the passion of his young manhood have its way. The look in her father's eyes told him that he'd better keep his self control.

The girl and her father had escaped after the Great War, and crossed the ocean as steerage passengers. They had become squatters like Crennie. When the girl's father had lain stricken that first terrible winter, Crennie took them meat and wild honey. In the spring, when the old man knew he was dying, he worried about what to do with the girl. At the end, in a desperate move, he said to Crennie, "You take good care of her and Caroline Rosalee will be your wife."

Now, as Crennie sat in a euphoric state, surrounded by the sweetnes of bird songs and the softness of the morning's perfumes, his hard eyes took on a tender look. For a moment, life itself took on a kind of beauty he had never known. He was sorry he had whipped Caroline for letting the pups stray into the bush to be taken by the animals. He had still been in a rage at one of the horses after it crowded him into the boards and he beat it mercilessly with a chain. The next morning Caroline was gone. He heard that she was somewhere in the city and that one woman in Buttonwood knew where she was. He had never given up on the idea of finding her when he got enough money. Now he would have it.

When the lawyer and the man with the badge on his cap came out the first time, the man said that the area was a Carolinian region. Crennie thought they were making fun of him because Caroline had left him and he drove them off with his skunk club. Later, the lawyer had him sign off any rights to the land. The mailman would bring the money out on his weekly run, the lawyer said.

As Crennie approached the road he looked over toward the tulip tree for the mailman's rig, but what he saw was a shiny new automobile. He approached it with some trepidation.

"Mr. Crennie?" the well-dressed man asked.

"I am."

"My name is Buckley," the young man said. "I'm here from the London Registry Office. By the strangest coincidence I was at the front of the Office when Mr. Black, the lawyer came in to search the title to this holding."

"It's a farm." Crennie said. "I made it into a farm!"

"There is no evidence that any individual has ever been registered as the owner of this parcel of land since the Crown made it available." Buckley stated. "When we made the discovery Mr. Black commented, 'It looks as though this land belongs to the first person who gets his name in this book.' I am that person, Mr. Crennie!"

"You bastard! You thieving bastard -- you stole my land!"

"Speaking of stealing," Buckley continued, "Did you know that Mr. Brome died in prison for stealing a loaf of bread and a pound of bacon? He died behind bars like a trapped animal! You see, my mother watched him slowly die. She watched her own brother die in jail!"

"I didn't mean to...."

Buckley stepped into the car. "You may stay on for a few weeks if you like," he called through the open window. "The Brome blood still carries a degree of compassion!"

Crennie slowly stepped onto the track. He looked around to see the car pulling away, then his eyes turned back to the bush, and he felt for the first time that he would never get free of it. His lungs burned as he dragged himself through the open spaces and beneath the canopies. He'd be alright if he could get to the gate, he told himself. Every step became a desperate effort. Three hours passed before he finally saw the gate ahead. He staggered the last few steps and grasped the gate post to steady himself. He threw off his dirty cap and tried to take a deep breath, but his lungs would not take the air.

Suddenly a massive pain exploded through his chest, sending him to the ground. He rolled onto his side as the blood came into his throat. He could see the fifteen vultures circling slowly over the edge of the tobacco. In his approaching delirium he was glad to see them. As the blood gushed from his mouth his eyes blurred. He could not see the young vultures already picking at the red stream running down the yellow sand toward the tobacco. Then Caroline came to him. She put her hand on his forehead and told him that she had come home and everything would be alright. He didn't know that the hand he felt on his shoulder was the great talons of the heavy vulture. It locked into position to ensure precise aim for the hooked hammer on the end of its ugly, poised neck. Before the first shattering blow struck his skull, Crennie was dead.

It was a week before they found him. When the doctor went out to declare him dead, the bones had been picked clean. Two young vultures, still too heavy to lift off, sent out vomiting growls from their choking gullets as they lumbered amongst the tobacco plants.

"What killed him, Doc?" asked the boy who now drove the aging man on the longer trips into the country.

"His life, Matt," the doctor said, leaving the boy, who wanted to be a doctor puzzled.

A light drizzle had started by the time they got out to the road. The old doctor turned and looked back at the darkening wilderness which now claimed the bones of Elmo Crennie.

"They say he wasn't civilized, Doc," the boy said. "Was he Doc?"

Cornered

I was ten years old the day Ed asked me to go with him to dig out a den of skunks. Right away thoughts of the smell were up against the excitement in Ed's skunk-hunting stories. The smell might have won out, except that I remembered about the watermelons. Ed had always let me have a few cents for picking melons to sell to the Saturday and Sunday people who came out from town, so I figured I had better not refuse him. And I knew he'd give me a little toward the secondhand bicycle in the window of the Buttonwood Hardware. That alone seemed reason enough for going.

As we headed out across the wide, snowy fields toward the scrub at the edge of the bush, my mind went ahead to the berry bushes where the women picked thimbleberries in August. Even with the briars catching your skin, there was something warm and good about berry picking, listening to the women and girls telling their secret thoughts about men. But now the little pellets ripped off the snow crust by the icy wind and hurled at my face like a thousand point-first needles quickly took my mind off berry picking. I put my head down and started concentrating on how to walk on the crust without sinking to my knees every other step, wasting a lot of energy I'd need for digging.

"They won't be out on a day like this," Ed said. "They'll all be down there sleeping together where it's warm. They won't be expecting us!" It was a little game Ed had with the skunks. I could see he was enjoying it even before he got there and as we approached the berry bushes his step and his talk both got faster.

"I've been watching their tracks every few days --
there's a lot of them down there," he said, as he cut
away the berry bushes with his shovel. I guessed that he
was counting on having enough pelt money left over to
get some whiskey from the bootlegger. That seemed to
be just as important to him as the things he needed. He
always said he thought of it as a reward for the unusual
and distasteful work he had to do to get money to live
on. He thought he should be rewarded quite often it
seemed to me!

"Now you can start with the pick, Matt," he said,
after he had moved back the snow. "There'll only be a
few inches of frost. I'll save my strength for the fast
digging near the end when the danger gets close. I don't
want to get you sprayed. Your mother wouldn't like it if
I brought you home all stunk up!"

I started swinging the pick-axe at the frosty earth and
I soon forgot about the cold. I even had to take off my
heavy coat. I knew there was no danger of getting
sprayed yet, so I went right at it, especially after Ed told
me that I was as good as any man he'd ever hired to
help him. Still, I knew that most men wouldn't come
within miles of one of Ed's skunk dens. Even my older
brother, Frank, had refused him that morning, saying his
friend Stan was coming out from town to show him the
new telephone truck. But I knew the main reason Frank
refused him was because he couldn't stand the smell.
He'd even throw up going past Ed's place on the way to
school if Ed had caught a new batch of skunks and the
smell was strong. The girls walking with us made fun of
Frank when he threw up. They said he'd never amount
to anything if he was that weak. I worried about that,
thinking Frank might be left out of things when he got
older. Maybe he wouldn't even get married because the
girls would all know about skunk smell making him
throw up.

As Ed watched my work he rolled a big wad of tobacco around in his mouth, spitting far off to the side. "Don't want to get any juice down the hole," he stated. "That would get them real upset." I couldn't figure how the smell of tobacco juice could get anything as stinky as skunks upset, but he said it would, so it must be right, I thought.

"I'll spell you a bit," he said, taking the shovel from me. In no time he was going at it real hard. His nose was running a kind of thread that fell down on the shovel handle and froze. Tobacco juice was dripping from the corners of his mouth. His great, strong arms lifting up the big loads of dirt made me think of the old steam shovel digging gravel from the dry river bed in summer. Suddenly he stopped digging. He hunched over and turned his ear to the hole. His breath started coming in fast, short puffs. "We're getting close," he warned, "Be ready with my club!" I picked the skunk club out of the bushes and held it out, trying not to let it shake too much. He dropped the club down beside him and continued to dig toward the den.

"There's the first one!" he yelled, as the tip of the tail of a skunk showed through the den opening. "Stand back!" he commanded. His hand sprang out like a cat's paw and in a lightning-fast move he yanked the skunk out and brought the club down in a crushing blow to its skull. He sent the skunk flying out of the hole spinning like a roman candle spraying out a yellow, juicy fog in every direction. I jumped back but it was too late, for some of the spray had caught my overalls, and some landed on my coat in the bushes. I choked for a few seconds until I got used to the smell. I wondered how a skunk with its head smashed in could keep on spraying. I figured it must have been something like the reflex in the bee stingers that Old Engleheart used to tell us about. He'd come around each year with a buggy load of clover honey that sent its sweetness swelling out into the air, flavouring everything around. He said that after the bee stung and left the barbed stinger in your arm, the muscles on the venom sacs kept pulsing, pumping the venom into you. And that's why you scrape the stinger off sideways with a fingernail or something instead of pulling it out and squeezing the venom sacs. I couldn't figure how nature thought it would do either the bees or the skunks any good to have reflex action working after they were dead. Then it struck me that it was strange for me to be thinking of skunks and honey bees at the same time. But it was stranger still to get an unexpected feeling for the skunks. It seemed almost unfair to get them cornered and then club them when they didn't have what you'd call a fair chance. But then I thought, when you go to kill a pig, it's cornered too, and it hasn't got any chance.

Ed was cornered in his own way by the big, deep scar across his chin, which showed up a lot more now with the tobacco juice running down over it. I had seen the hurt in his eyes sometimes when he ran his hand over it after people had looked at him like he was something less than they were. Some said he got the scar in a fight in a bootlegging joint in Detroit when he went across one night while he was working on the big tunnel under the river. Frank told me he thought Ed started skunk hunting because people's looks told him that's all he was good for. But I couldn't see how anybody who had worked on the big tunnel could ever come down to something as low as skunk hunting. I thought something should have been done to fix up the scar so it wouldn't look so bad, but most people seemed to think Ed deserved the scar and that's the way it should stay.

"Number two!" Ed yelled with urgency in his voice. But this time it didn't work quite right, because the skunk got its tail up too fast and let go before Ed could yank it out and bring down the club. It didn't bother Ed much. He just wiped the yellow juice off his face with the back of his hand and went about giving that skunk a few extra smashing blows to the skull.

In less than five minutes there were seven skunks cooling in the snow. Ed stood back looking at them. "Two prime out of seven," he said. "Two without a smidgeon of white. They'll bring a good price!" he added, smiling and winking at the same time. I knew he could already feel the extra money in his hands for the whiskey. "I'll skin them at home," he said, swinging the heavy sack over his shoulder.

As I walked away from Ed's place and headed for home in the approaching dusk, I felt the good that comes from accomplishing something with your own hands. I knew that I'd soon have a quarter for helping Ed, and I could see the bicycle almost within reach. It was still in my mind when I started up our lane in the half dark. It was then that I spotted Stan's shiny, red telephone truck sitting in the yard and that fancy truck put the bicycle right out of my head.

There was nobody around, so I quietly opened the door and got in just to see what it felt like. Soon any thoughts of the day's skunk hunting seemed a million miles away. There was something on the dash that looked like the dial on a radio in the hardware store window. I didn't think it would do any harm, so I started experimenting with the knobs. Out came the sound of a guitar and a man singing something about a 'great speckled bird'. After that there was a girl singing, 'Oh, Johnny, how you can love'. It was just when she was ending the word 'love' that the door of the house swung open and Frank and Stan started strutting toward the truck. I could hear Stan bragging that he had to hurry back to town to take Viola to the show. Then they saw me. I knew Stan was mad just because I was in the truck. He yanked open the door, and I expected him to say, "What are you doing in my truck?", but he only got as far as "What...?" before he started to choke. He wheeled and stumbled away from the truck. Then Frank started to throw up his supper. I jumped out and ran behind the corn crib and tried to think of something to do, but I couldn't come up with anything.

"We'll leave the doors open to the cold and it will be alright in a couple of days," Frank called to Stan who was already heading for town at a fast clip.

What happened in town between Stan and Viola that night has to be guessed, at least partly. Frank told me years later that Viola seemed skeptical about the skunk story, and Stan got flustered and changed his story about why he didn't have the truck. That's where Stan made a real mistake because those blue eyes of Viola's were the kind that were on the lookout for the truth. I found that out the next day when Viola rode her bicycle out to our place in the cold to see if the truck was there. Frank let her in just as my mother got me located with my bare back to the oven of the kitchen stove to drive the cold out. Viola was so pretty with her long, black hair and special eyes, that I almost wanted to run and hide. She didn't say much to me, but she talked with Frank for quite a while. A blizzard blew up and her father came to get her. He told Viola to leave the bicycle and said something about a new bicycle in the spring. I figured they were giving it to us without really saying so because they didn't want to let on about our being poor.

I thought about the skunk hunting adventure with Ed when the phone call came for me yesterday here at the hospital.

"His heart?" I asked.

"No," Frank replied. "They figure he froze to death. They found him propped up against a small tree where he had been digging. He had been doing well recently, with the big jump in the price of pelts, and he had plenty of money for whiskey. There was still some in the bottle lying beside him. It looked as though he was taking a rest and fell asleep. His mackinaw was spread out over the berry bushes a few feet away."

As I sat listening, my mind flashed back over all the things that seemed to have happened to people's lives because I went skunk hunting with Ed that one time. I thought about Viola and her two children with the same kind of truth-searching eyes as hers. I see them every year or two when I go back. And I thought of Stan, somewhere in the outback of Australia, driving his landrover through the scrub across the moonlit desert, looking for kangaroos to show the tourists. He couldn't live in his hometown knowing that Viola had married somebody else he said. And I thought about the unlikelihood of my becoming a doctor if I hadn't become friends with the old town doctor. They had to call him for me after I got near-pneumonia from staying out in the cold barn so long with pails of hot water and strong soap, trying to get the smell off so I could go into the house. He said life was a fight, and that I had better start fighting right then. And he said he'd help me become a doctor if I showed some spunk. It would give him a day off now and then, he argued. That offer was like a command when I was lying there so weak, and I was never able to get my mind completely free of it, even after I got better.

"If you can get away from that hospital long enough to get down for the funeral, we'd like you to come for supper," Frank said. "But please...no story about skunk hunting with Ed. It would be almost certain to get Viola going again on how her life 'might have been altogether different'!"

The Min-Min Light

"Reginald, will you put the kettle on please? I can see the Tapps' car lights over the ridge beyond Wild Creek."

Kate Grimshaw went to the pantry to get some cake. Lucky there's a good lot of the cake left, she thought, as she lifted the lid from the large dish. In the early days the rats would have had their share of that cake. She smiled and put the heavy lid back. She'd be glad to see the neighbours. It had been almost three months since their last visit.

Reginald Grimshaw went to the window and peered into the darkness. "No sign of them yet Kate," he said. "It wasn't a bit of lightning or something you saw?"

"No, and it wasn't the mating light in the kangaroos' eyes! I know a car light when I see one. It was about two miles over, I'd say. They'll be here soon."

Reginald Grimshaw opened the door and took a few steps into the yard. The quiet air of evening was uneasy with static charge lingering from the day-long dust storm. It was a time, he thought, to be on the look-out for the Min-Min -- that strange ball of light which skipped erratically over the ground for several minutes before it suddenly disappeared. The Aborigines spoke of it often and when one of them spotted a Min-Min on a walk-about, they'd get a corroberee going and dance and sing until daylight. They were a superstitious lot! 'I see Min-Min -- time for baby' the old aboriginal woman had said to his mother on the night of his birth. 'Min-Min when baby come -- Min-Min when old man go to long dreamtime!'

"Kate, I'm getting worried," Reginald said, returning to the kitchen. "They should be here by now. I wonder if they could have gone off the track at Wild Creek, or run into a rock at the gap...there have been some slips there lately. I think we'd better take a look."

"Oh, Dorothy and Jim have crossed as many creeks as we have! Their lights are probably hidden in the mulga. I'll get the bed ready...they'll be staying for the night."

"Kate, I've got an itchiness something's wrong. And that air feels like a storm. I'm going to have a look."

She watched him through the door. There was no point in trying to stop him. He still had the stubbornness which had kept them going when the dingoes ran them out of sheep and when the droughts had scattered the dried-up carcasses of their cattle across five thousand acres. But behind his lean, leathered face was kindness for her, and for the Aboriginal stockmen. He understood when they needed to go on their walkabouts. He never hurried them out of their dreamtimes. She listened now as he called Jimmy and Charlie, his two most trusted Aboriginal boys. Then the land rover's engine faded behind the mulga bushes. She thought of the times he had volunteered to look for a lost stockman, or for strangers from the city who never seemed to understand the dangers of the outback. Sometimes they'd find them before the blinding heat had sucked all the water from their bodies. But there were times when they found only bleached bones huddled under a tree. She worried about his going out at night, now that he was nearing seventy.

"Well boys," Reginald remarked, as they approached the creek, "There's no sign of a car down there at the billabong."

"Look! Look!" Jimmy shouted, bouncing up and down on the seat as their lights fell on a big, grey kangaroo lying by the pool. "Kanga lie down -- new joey maybe!"

"Easy boys! We won't disturb her." Reginald focussed his glasses. "The joey is almost to the pouch!"

"Joey!" Jimmy's eyes bulged with excitement as he glanced at Charlie. "I get joey!" And with that he was out of the land rover and racing toward the kangaroo.

"He gonna eat joey!" Charlie said excitedly. "He never eat joey before!"

The race for the joey was an aboriginal custom and Reginald never interfered. But the thought of crunching the embryonic organism between the teeth still made him nauseous, even after so many years.

The kangaroo, mesmerized by the lights, remained calm until Jimmy was just about to snatch the joey. Then she bounded away into the bush with Jimmy chasing after her.

"He'll get lost. Come back!" Reginald shouted. But Jimmy heard nothing save his own screams of delight which soon became muffled in the mulga bushes.

"There's a storm on the way," Reginald said. "We're in a bit of trouble now, I think." He waited a few minutes hoping Jimmy would return, then headed the rover back toward the Aborigines' lodgings. "Tell Ben we'll search at daylight," he instructed Charlie. "Then tell Mrs. Grimshaw that I have gone up to the Gap to look for our neighbours."

Reginald eased the rover over the track and up the bank of Wild Creek. He stopped and shouted as loudly as he could, then listened, but he heard only the sounds of the rising wind and distant thunder. He jumped into the rover and turned it toward Dingo Gap.

"So that's it, is it?" he said out loud, as a three foot boulder showed up in his head lights at the far end of the gap. "They've had to turn back...a bit of a shame after battling the track for twenty-five miles. I'll drag this critter out of the way." He quickly looped a chain around the boulder and started to winch it forward just as a torrential downpour began. "Damn! I'd better get this thing to one side and get out of here," he called urgently to himself as the water rose rapidly to his ankles. On his third frantic attempt to reposition the chain his ear caught the sound of crashing boulders and the roar of rushing water. He leapt to a small ledge seconds before a massive wave slammed into the land rover tumbling it end over end, its lights throwing arcs to the sky. He searched for a higher ledge in the lightning flashes, then made a daring leap across a deep crevasse. He dug his fingers into the rough slope of a huge table rock and scrambled to its top. Where would Jimmy be, he wondered...buried in some lonely stream bed? Sudden storms in the outback had often caught people in massive flows of water roaring down dry stream beds with the speed of an express train. Sometimes neither they nor their vehicles were ever seen again, having been crushed under hundreds of tons of rocks and mud. But *he* shouldn't have gotten into this fix...*he* knew of the danger. He stretched out on the great rock near a deep split which thousands of years of expansion and contraction had fashioned, leaving the huge monolith in two almost equal hemispheres. Suddenly he felt a chill and his mind was not focussing well. He wondered about the unusual feeling in his chest.

I'll see better at the top," Ben called back to Charlie, as he struggled over the rusty-red rocks. He swung his keen eyes over the boulders and into the crevices searching for some sign of Reginald Grimshaw. Suddenly his eyes fell upon what appeared to be a stockman's hat flattened on a rock below. He narrowed his gaze into the deep crevasse. "Charlie!" he yelled excitedly, his voice echoing through the gorge. "I see Papa-boss! Quick, bring the rope!"

"Papa-boss is dead! Papa-boss is dead!" the boy muttered, standing motionless beside the horses.

"Charlie!" Ben said sharply, "Bring the rope from my saddle!" He made his way to the deep split in the rock and peered down to where Reginald Grimshaw lay perfectly still, his pale face to the sky.

"Maybe he's alive!" Ben said encouragingly. "You can go down. Bring that pole the storm brought...we'll have to jack him up." He lowered the boy on the rope and instructed him in making a sling.

"Alive!" the boy shouted, when he noticed a slight movement in the man's chest.

"Good on ya, Charlie! Come up here quick -- we'll get him out. She'll be right!" They put the pole through a sliding loop in the rope, and using a small boulder as a fulcrum began to lift the man carefully toward the top.

"There's more than one way to trick a dingo mate!" Ben said, winking at the boy.

"Move that mob slowly boys -- it's a long way to Victoria," the elderly man whispered coarsely as he opened his eyes for a moment at the top.

"Crazy?" Charlie asked.

"He's remembering the old days," Ben explained.

"Gooday!" the dogger greeted, as he walked toward the door. "I picked up something that may belong on this station."

"Not a dead dingo?" Kate Grimshaw questioned.

"A lot better than that -- a real live boy. He's asleep in the rover. 'Jimmy', I think that's his name. I'll fetch him if he's yours."

"Jimmy!" Kate Grimshaw hurried to the sleeping boy. "We thought the storm got...Oh, I must tell Reginald!"

"I found him under a bush when I was trailing a dingo. He couldn't talk with his tongue so swelled. After a little water made him right, he kept whispering something until I finally made out what I thought to be 'Jimmy' and 'Wild Creek'. Then he fell asleep. It was a bit of luck I spotted him, I'd say. I happened along just as some dingoes broke a cattle ring. I shot two that were grabbing at the calves. The rest scattered, but not before I tagged their lean, red leader. I didn't want him suffering so I followed him into the bush. He's not suffering anymore!"

"If you'll take the boy to the lodgings, I'll put the kettle on. Come right into the kitchen when you're through." Kate Grimshaw hurried to the house. She turned quickly toward Reginald's room, then stopped. It would be better to wait until he was fully awake, she decided.

"I'll tell Reginald the good news when he wakes up," she stated, as she filled the dogger's large tin cup with hot tea. He's been terribly down since the accident. It will give him a boost."

"Reginald? Reginald Grimshaw?" the dogger queried.

"Goodness! I haven't even introduced myself. I'm Kate Grimshaw."

"I heard of the accident on the women's galah session this morning. I listen sometimes -- it helps me find the trouble spots."

"The galah news travels faster than a red 'roo'!" she remarked. "It was only yesterday when the radio cleared that I told the Tapps about Reginald. We *are* a bit like galahs, I guess. Still, it's good that we women can stay in touch. Of course, the women talk a lot of nonsense nowadays, but we don't lose them to isolation like we used to."

"Thanks for the tucker," the dogger said, his finger tip to his hat. "There's no better cake in the outback, I reckon! I'll be hurrying along -- there's a bad time with the dingoes on some sheep stations to the north. With the new grass springing from the rain and enough stock, the owners can look to a good year, that is, if we can get on top of the dingoes!"

Kate Grimshaw poured a cup of fresh tea and walked toward the bedroom. "Reginald? Are you awake?"

"How long has it been since the dogger brought Jimmy home?" Reginald asked. "It's a week, isn't it?"

"It's ten days. And it's time you had some visitors. Dorothy and Jim Tapp are coming tomorrow evening. They'll be glad to get away, Dorothy said. They've not been off the station in three months."

"The Min-Min light won't fool us this time, Kate. Are you sure it wasn't a bit of lightning or something?"

"Have your tea and try to rest for the visit."

The next morning Kate was in her kitchen two hours before daylight baking a cake. She expected the doctor from Broken Hill to land in the lower paddock at day-break with the new equipment to check Reginald's heart. She had just taken the large cake from the oven when there was a loud, sporadic knocking at the door. She hurried to answer it.

"Min-Min!" Jimmy burst out. "Min-Min!"

"What? What's wrong?"

"Min-Min!" the boy cried, gesturing wildly.

Kate's eyes focussed on the ball of light bouncing erratically toward Wild Creek. She started to call Reginald, then hesitated when she thought of the possible danger in waking him suddenly. But he'd be fully awake now...the aroma of fresh cake baking always did bring him from his sleep. She hurried to his bedroom.

"Reginald, come quickly and see the Min-Min light!" She opened the door to the darkened room. "Reginald? Reginald...?"

Katerina

"Katerina!" Theresa called from the kitchen. "Katerina, come and carry the cabbage rolls. Your gentleman will be starved before we get supper on the table!"

"Excuse me, Bart," Katherine said, hurrying to the kitchen. "Theresa! Please don't call me Katerina in Bart's presence. I told him my name is Katherine. You know how some men feel about the old names!"

"Men don't care what women call themselves. They think more about what's on the table," Theresa remarked offhandedly, turning to the dining room. "Isn't that right, sir?"

"I...suppose there's some truth in that," Bart replied, casting a quick glance at Katherine.

"Gotta remember your roots, girl!" Theresa reminded Katherine, as she placed a steaming bowl of borscht before Bart. "Anyway, Oran always called you Katerina when he wanted to be nice to you and put you on a pedestal. And your mother did it too!"

Katherine sat alone in her kitchen waiting for the kettle to boil. She thought about Theresa calling her 'Katerina' at supper. It had embarrassed her in front of Bart, the only man she had taken any interest in since Oran's death, and the only man who had shown any interest in her.

It was true -- her mother had often called her Katerina when she wanted to make her feel special. 'Katerina, you can help me make the borscht'...'Katerina, you can have the red ribbon for your pretty hair'...'Katerina, you helped to save your father's life!'

"Sam! Dad?" She could still hear Mike's voice ringing out from the top of the valley high above the river.

It was a beautiful winter day. Sam had come over early that morning as he did every Sunday morning, because he was lonesome, her mother said.

"We'll go," her father said to Sam and her. "Pyrohy, no church for us. Let them talk in the church about the fishes. We'll catch a real one! You, me and Sam." He didn't like the priest anyway. He was like the foreman in the city foundry where he had worked, he said, except that you could get away from the foreman sometimes. But you could never get away from that priest. He'd be in your life every second of the day if you let him.

They rode the seven miles to the great river beyond the hills, with the sleigh making happy, squeaky sounds on the hard-frozen snow. The time went by quickly and the cold didn't matter because the nest in the hay kept them warm. The jingling bells on the horse made a special kind of music to go with the good songs Sam and her father sang after they drank from the bottle. She liked to hear the songs, especially the ones Sam sang, because you could almost see and feel what he was singing about: galloping the horses across the steppes of the old country, doing the wild dances in bright costumes.

"Two hours!" her father exclaimed. "That's how long we've got to fish after we chop through the thick ice on the river. Sam will make the fire, I will chop the ice, you fish Katerina." They tied the horse to a small spruce behind a bluff of poplars, out of the wind. Then they half-slid down the steep side of the valley toward the river below.

"I want to toast sandwiches," the eight-year old girl said, as she took her father's hand and pretended she was skate-dancing down the snow-crusted slope. Her father was all hers this day. She was glad that there was no room on the sleigh for the other kids.

"Better than listening to the Father, eh?" her father said, enjoying the freedom and the warm feeling in his belly from the moonshine.

Better than anything in the world, she thought, as she tightened her grip on his hand. She knew that he enjoyed her. And she knew that he had treated her in a special way ever since the time her mother had taken her to stay with the neighbours when Theodore got sick. When she came home Theodore was gone. She cried...she didn't know why. They all said he had gone to a good place and wouldn't be sick any more. But she and her baby brother had always played together, and he would play whatever she wanted to play. '*You* are our baby now,' they told her.

Chop! Chop! Chop! The crack of the axe against the flint-hard ice rifled through the frosty air and echoed sharply from the wide banks of the river, down to the big bend and back again.

"I show her how to fish," Sam said proudly. He baited the hook with a piece of pork rind and dropped the line down the hole to the bottom, then lifted it a foot and tied a red yarn on the line at ice level. "Jiggle it a little, Katerina -- might wake up fish if he's close!"

How she'd like to catch a fish to take home like her father did sometimes. She was sure there were lots of them down there. Her teacher told them of the great fish in the big rivers and how they swam away up the river to lay their eggs in a quiet place so they could hatch in the sand and gravel. The fish were not very active in the winter, the teacher said. She would make sure any that were near would see the bait. She jiggled it up and down every few seconds. She could hear her father and Sam singing and laughing by the fire, but she could think of nothing but the great, beautiful fish which she was sure was watching her bait, moving closer each time she jiggled it. After a half hour, when there was no bite on her hook, she began to think that the fish were all asleep somewhere, maybe in a quiet spot down by the big bend. And the cold was starting to make her want to pee.

"Daddy, I've got to go behind the bushes," she called.

"Alright, my little pyrohy. I'll fish till you come back. If one wants to get on the hook, I'll tell him to wait for you!" Then he laughed the way he always did when he was making a joke. And Sam laughed too. The strong drink was making it easy for them to laugh, and as Sam's voice got louder she heard him starting to tell about the time he went from the city out to the valley.

"I sing you a song, Taras," he said, slapping her father on the shoulder. "I sing you a song me and old George sing when we go out to the long valley to grow sunflowers in the hot summer. We leave Marishka in the city -- no place for her in valley. I get awful lonely. George, he get lonely too, but not the same like me. He got no woman, and he gettin' old. Sometimes we sing just to make feel better. Make fun song. Use own names. George say some. I say some. Songs kinda crazy, but better crazy songs than go crazy!"

He leaned back and looked up at the sky, then began to sing the new words to the tune of the old Russian folk song he sang sometimes. He sang it in a way that made it seem as though it must have been right in his blood when he was born, and he never had to learn it at all.

'Old George say to Sam,
Y ou better mix-em-up da gears
And get machine a'workin'
Or we be here four years,
And never get no sunflowers
What grows in dis land,

And never get da bowl of borscht
From sweet Marishka's hand...'

For a moment Sam seemed to be back in the warm sun planting sunflowers, as he threw his head back and laughed. Then he was quiet, and his face began to look sad. She knew that he was starting to think about Marishka again, like he did sometimes when he was talking to her dad and mother. They didn't know she could hear the things about sin and the curse the priest talked about. One time at night when they thought she was asleep, she heard her mother tell her father that she had been thinking about poor Marishka out there alone in the graveyard, and about Marishka asking her if it was a sin to want to die. When her mother told Marishka it wasn't a sin, Marishka took rat poison because she knew that she would never have any children. But Sam never knew about the rat poison. Nobody else did. Her mother buried the tin the day she found Marishka.

Sam picked up the bottle and stared out across the wide river. "But George gone. Marishka gone. Goddam! Goddam! Goddam! I tell her we go back, grow cabbages and sunflowers where warm, but she say no, it be alright. But she die and leave me. Forty-one! Goddam! Goddam! Goddam!" He lifted the bottle to his mouth and drank deeply.

"Take one," he said, after he caught his breath.

"Better not. Get late," her father replied.

She could hear her father's talk getting like Sam's, the way it did quite often when they were drinking. She thought it was because he was trying to show Sam that he was still his friend.

The two men leaned back against the black-green spruce boughs they had piled in a half circle in front of the fire and Sam was soon asleep. Then her father went to sleep too.

"I've got one!" Katerina yelled, and she quickly pulled the line through the thin ice forming over the

75

hole. She got the big pike to where she could see his great jaws. She was afraid to get her fingers behind his gills to pull him out the way her father did. She struggled to hold the line tight, waiting for help, afraid to take her eyes off the fish. Then the fish made a lightning-fast move ripping the line from her numbing hands and sending a splash of icy water onto her face. For a moment she lost her breath. She began to cry, then caught herself, remembering her mother's words: 'You never cry in cold...face freeze...you not pretty anymore!' She turned to the shore and called to her father. Then she went and shook him, but he just grunted and kept on sleeping. She put more wood on the fire and crowded close to the red flames. They'll wake up soon, she told herself. The heat warmed her face and made her sleepy. She wanted to lie down beside them but she knew they should be going home.

The icy pellets of snow which struck her face like sharp needles woke her from the short sleep into which the warmth of the fire had tricked her. She sat up quickly, wondering where she was. Sam's snoring and the low moans coming from her father soon reminded her that they were still at the river. The wind was rising rapidly. It made the dead branches of the burned-over jack pines and spruces saw against each other, creating an eerie kind of music like she read about in a story at school. Darkness was falling over the woods, and she could no longer see across the river.

She ran over to her father and shook him awake, but he stayed awake only long enough to say that he was sick and to put some more wood on the fire. She hurried to gather all the pieces of wood not too heavy, and piled them close to the fire. Then she got a frozen beef sandwich from the bag and laid it near the fire. There was no use in trying to give her father anything to eat. He never ate when he drank a lot. She chewed the half-frozen meat and bread, then went behind the poplars to pee before piling most of the wood on the fire.

Sam's big fur coat was open over his great belly and she could not get it up over him because he was lying on the part with the button holes. She buttoned up her father's coat and pushed the spruce boughs around him and Sam, making a kind of pit. Then the icy blizzard drove her into the shelter with them. She pulled a few boughs over top of them as the early darkness of winter closed the big valley off from the rest of the world. She got as close to her father as she could get and put her head against his hot face. The stinking, sour smell turned her away for a moment, but then she thought of her father lifting her up and hugging her lots of times when his breath was like that, and she moved back close to him. She thought of the horse, still tied to the tree in the bluff of poplars far up at the top of the valley. She hoped that the big fur blanket made from the cow that died last winter would keep him warm. It must be lonely for him up there, she thought.

The blizzard screamed at her to stay awake and to go to sleep. She could hear the tall, dead spruces and jack pines cracking like rifles and then crashing to the ground. Soon the roar of the icy wind shut out everything but itself. The sound it made through the spires of the dead trees was like a thousand screams of people, from babies to old men and women. Then she dreamt about the fish, the icons in the church, the prince that was made out of a frog, and the jelly beans at the school Christmas party.

When Katerina opened her eyes the steel-blue sky was showing through the holes in the snow-covered spruce boughs. Her father's arm was around her and he was mumbling something. For a moment she wondered if she was really awake. Was she having a bad dream like she did sometimes after church?

"Pyrohy, tell Sam to make a fire," her father said in a coarse whisper. Then he started to snore again, but it sounded more like a gargle. She pushed back the boughs for more light and gently shook him awake again. There was a trace of blood on his mouth and his face was grey. She brushed the crusted snow from his fur hat and pushed it up so she could see his eyes. They were like the hard glass fruit bowl where her mother hid the money.

"I'll be better when I get warm. Tell Sam to make a fire," her father mumbled. She put her face down against his. Her warm tears shocked him into a better consciousness. "Pyrohy," he whispered. "My pyrohy!"

"I will," she said. "I'll wake up Sam to do the fire." She crawled out from under the snow-heavy spruce boughs and looked at Sam. He was still asleep. But he didn't seem asleep because his big belly wasn't moving up and down like it was when she tried to button his coat. His one bare hand lay across his leg as though it was trying to protect it from the cold. But it was a funny colour, like skim milk, only with less colour. She touched his hand to wake him. It was hard and cold. Then she looked at his face. It too was like skim milk, and his thick, black moustache had ice in it, and even his eye lashes had ice on them.

"Mr. Sam," she said, in a frightened half-cry, "are you sick? Mr. Sam, please wake up and make a fire. Daddy's sick, and it's daylight now."

She turned back to her father. "He won't wake up. I'll make a fire with your matches," she said in quick succession, trying to allay any suspicion her father might have that something was wrong. Afraid to think dead -- afraid to say dead.

"The matches are in a tin box in Sam's pocket. Maybe Sam needs more time to sleep it off. He took maybe too much...we shouldn't bring three bottles."

She carefully stepped toward the great, round man lying stiff and still, and wondered which pocket the matches were in. She was afraid to touch him. Was this the curse the priest talked about? Because Sam didn't go to church? And didn't believe in the blood or something? She tried the large pocket with the flap, then the smaller pockets. Then her shaking hands tried to pull the other coat pocket from under the massive body. Maybe I can roll him enough to pull out the part he's on, she reasoned, but her tiny frame was no match for the two hundred and fifty pounds of Sam's rigid body.

She wanted to cry, run away, and call her mother all at the same time. And her feet were burning. And the cold was biting her face and making its way through her clothes. She wasn't the spoiled brat the kids at school said she was either! She'd like to see *them* move Sam over -- especially that Olga Vorkapitch who was so stuck up. She could see Olga whispering to Sonja when the teacher wasn't looking.

"Spoiled brat! Spoiled brat! Can't even lift a pussy cat!"

"I can too!" she shouted angrily, holding back the tears. "Bastard! Bastard Sonja! That's what you are. The boys all call you that, too." She picked up the ball bat and stood facing the enemy, which quickly dissolved into the snow-covered ice of the river. As her mind recovered from the half-faint and came back to her, she found her hands tightly clenched around a long, black-burned spruce pole. I'll get it underneath him and roll him over like daddy does when he cuts the trees, she thought. She pushed the pole through the boughs and worked it under Sam's wide shoulder. Then she moved out to the end of the pole and began to lift. She worried that it might slip and hurt his face. She thought she might be hurting him all over. She shut her eyes and lifted as hard as she could. Suddenly the weight came off the pole. She opened her eyes to see Sam lying face down in the snow. She waited a few seconds to see if he might come alive and move. Then she raced to the pocket and snatched the matches before anything could happen. She gathered some dead spruce boughs and shook off the snow. Then she picked up some broken pieces the storm had made in the night. She placed them together the way her father did, and lit a match to start the fire.

The warmth soon reached her father and he began to mutter some weak words. At first she couldn't make out what he was trying to say.

"Sam is dead..."

"Yes, daddy."

"I have to help now...I will get up," he said. But he could not raise himself.

She found sandwiches, toasted them, and ate. Then she waited. Her father slept a little each time after he tried to talk. She couldn't tell what he was trying to say anymore. Someone would come -- maybe her mother. She'd know what to do! Maybe her mother was looking for them high up the valley amongst the trees. She wanted to tell her father that someone was coming, and she almost did one time when he was conscious, just so he wouldn't worry and get sicker. The warm fire and the sandwiches made her sleepy. She sat down by her father and let her eyes close for a few seconds.

Something woke her...what was it? She waited -- listened. There was something behind the bushes where she had gone to pee. She pushed her parka hood back and cautiously let her eyes peek around the fur edge toward the sound. Two big, grey dogs were looking out from behind the bushes. But they didn't look like the dogs she knew. Maybe they were the wild dogs she had heard about. She turned to get a better look. The tall dogs moved a step closer and let their red tongues hang out between their teeth. One gave a low-sounding growl which she knew wasn't friendly. Then the other one growled and it was worse. Her backbone felt like a million needles had skated up it fast as lightning. For a moment she was paralyzed with fear. She tried to cry out, but she could not. Then the fear gave way to something inside her and she sprang to her feet to defend her father. She inched carefully toward the pole between her and the wolves, defiantly throwing her arms in their direction and yelling, "Go away! Go away! Go away!" as loudly as her young voice would let her and as threateningly as she knew how.

The wolves stood their ground without making any sound for a little while. Then they started their guttural growls again and their lips curled away from their large, white fangs.

Maybe if I give them a sandwich they'll go, she thought, stepping sideways to the sack by the edge of the fire. She drew out the frozen lump of three sandwiches which now came apart easily. She threw each one as far as she could beyond the wolves. Then she dashed to grab the pole and when the wolves turned around she was ready. They stood licking their lips and stretching their mouths wide until she moved toward them brandishing the long pole. Then they backed away, making low, guttural complaints as they started up the side of the valley.

It was a rifle! Twice! Then a third time! Then two more! Then a voice far up at the top!

"Sam! Dad? Where are you? Sam? Dad?"

Katerina started to run toward the voice, then caught herself and turned back. Her father...she couldn't leave him! She yelled in the strongest, most piercing voice of her life.

"Here! Here!" And the sound flew through the still, cold air across the ice of the great river and bounced back from the other side.

"Stay there! Stay there!" she heard from high up the river valley. And the echo: 'Stay there! Stay there! Stay there!'

Her sharpened senses told her it was Mike's voice. Why hadn't she thought about Mike finding them. Maybe it was because Mike was mean to her at times. He called her a spoiled brat, too. But that didn't matter now. And she would try to be good to him from now on, even if he did get nasty and say, 'The youngest one is always spoiled rotten -- and you're the one!' He'd even slap her behind when nobody was around. 'The rest can spoil you, but I won't,' he'd say, as his fast hand sent a message from her bottom to her head.

The tears she had held back so many times now came in a torrent. She cried and laughed at the same time and she peed her pants from holding it too long.

"Crying again? Still a spoiled brat!" Mike teased, as she wiped her runny nose on her sleeve. He picked her up in his strong, seventeen-year-old arms. He squeezed her and put a kiss against the tears. Then he put her down and looked over to see his father's grey face turned toward the sky, his stained mouth mumbling incoherently, as though trying to tell the world he was still a part of it. And Sam, stiff and cold, telling the world that he was no longer a part of it.

"The damn fools!" Mike said, looking at the empty bottles. "Drinking that rot-gut! Its got Sam. It'll get dad, too, some day. Maybe it's already got him! Can you hear me, dad?" he called, kneeling by his father. "Everything will be alright. We're going home. Old Kowalchuk's bringing the horse. He's unhooking the sleigh. We'll get Sam later -- if the wolves don't get him first!"

"Had to shoot two wolves up top, Katerina," Mike said. "The slinking bastards were just ready to get at the horse's throat. And that poor bastard tied to a tree. They'd have had a picnic!"

'What's the difference between a slinking bastard and a bastard like the horse, or Sonja? What's a bastard?' Katerina asked herself. She wanted to tell Mike that she had driven off two wolves herself, but she thought he wouldn't believe her. He knew that she exaggerated sometimes. Lied? Yes, sometimes if she really had to, but mostly she just made the thing bigger than it really was. She lied to the priest when she said she had bowed every night before the icon above her bed. But then, sometimes she bowed ten times in a row to make up for the times she missed. Anyway, they'd all find out about the wolves in time.

"You're a different man than you were a few days ago," the doctor said. "I tell you, Taras, another time or two like this, and it's the end for you! But you're going to pull through this time. Just a small lesion in your stomach. It'll get a lot bigger if you keep on!" The doctor sounded half angry and half sad when he was talking to her father. "There are enough things to kill you in this god-forsaken north country without you adding to them!" he grumbled, as he turned to come down the stairs where Katerina was waiting.

"He's alright. I guess you are, too. You look alright," he said, smiling, giving her thick, black hair a rub. "You've got something pretty special under that good hair!" She didn't know quite what he meant, but 'special' sounded as though it was good. Special! Am I different from the rest, she wondered. Maybe they'd let her go up and see her father now. She'd even bring down the pot and empty it if they wanted her to, just to get the chance to see her father. Maybe she wouldn't have to just listen at the bottom of the stairs when her mother was talking to her father after she had given him the thin soup the doctor said he could have.

"They wouldn't bury Sam in the church yard?"

"No, he wasn't a member," her mother explained.

"They didn't do the service in the church?"

"No, they did it in Kowalchuk's house," her mother answered.

"That damn priest! I built that church with my own hands. There'd be no church without my hands. Maybe we'd be better off!"

"Rest, my husband. Try to sleep."

"You know, if Marishka had had a baby they'd call it a bastard, like Sonja!" her father said, sounding angry.

"It would be whatever the priest said."

"He'll be gone some day, like Sam. Maybe there'll never be church bastards anymore!"

So that's what a bastard was, Katerina told herself. Sonja wasn't christened. Wolves aren't christened either. She wondered if she was.

It had taken until the last time she sat on her mother's bed as her mother lay dying, to discover that she had not been exorcised when she was a baby.

"We couldn't do it at the right time because of the bad flu, so it never got done," her mother explained, her voice shallow and faltering. "I got your father to take some of your hair to the priest to burn at the altar, but he said you had to be there or the bad spirits wouldn't come out." Her mother looked up at her and her eyes showed the soft determination they had always had.

"I want to die now, Katerina," she said softly. "Is it a sin to want to die?" She put her arms around her mother and wept a little as she said, "I love you mom!"

"No bad spirits. No sin. Just love," her mother whispered. And with that she closed her eyes. Her gentle grip on Katerina's hand slowly weakened, then was gone.

How like a dream a lot of it was now, Katherine thought, as she poured a cup of coffee and walked to the window. The full moon was just about to top the tall spruces. In a few seconds the quiet ocean below would turn to soft silver and she would think of the times Oran had stood beside her at the window he put there just for her. But time was forging a new reality and the certainties of that reality could not be ignored. She was forty-one. Oran had been dead for a year. Somehow she had survived. Bart had come along. And now, she thought, she might be at the turning point.

Dogwood

Elvira sat in her rocking chair on the open verandah in the freshness of the summer evening. She put the chair into a gentle rock, and her knitting fingers began to play a sweater game with the new baby in the distant city. As her fingers traced the map in her mind, she started thinking back on her life. The children and grandchildren would have been quite different if she had married Bert Watson, who lost a leg in the war. He had mostly always given her a ride home in his truck after she picked berries all day. Sometimes he had even given her a few cents a box for picking, besides the berries he gave her for her work. And he had always treated her like a lady! There was something good and deserving about him. It was even in his voice when he spoke.

She took off her hearing aid and slipped it in her pocket. Her husband would be out soon, his teeth already in the jar for the night, tobacco juice running from the corners of his mouth as he muttered something from time to time, even though he knew she couldn't hear without her hearing aid. He'd sit there, his wiry old body still as straight as the back of his chair. He'd look over once in a while and a little bit of a weasel grin would come around his mouth. She wondered why she had married him. Something seemed to have happened that day when she was touching the petals of the flowering dogwood, and she had given her promise. The dogwood always had made her lose her sense a little.

The old man finished shaving and combed his hair. He would surprise her this night. There had been something special about the apple pie she made from the tart red astrikhans the berry farmer brought her. He had not tasted a pie quite like that since the day his mother asked Elvira over for supper on her eighteenth birthday. After supper he had gone walking with her to see the dogwoods. She had surprised him when she accepted his proposal, and his heart pounded in anticipation of a life full of love. But she had kept herself distant from him a lot of the time. He wondered how he ever caught her enough times at the right time to get the three children. Still, she had taken good care of things. He felt unusually warm about her this evening. He'd try to show her how he felt. He had noticed at supper that she had her hair all done up, and with that pink summer dress around her small, plump body, she looked soft and warm.

She took no notice of him when he sat down on his straight chair. He wondered how to tell her that he felt warmly about her. Finally he leaned over and said, as plainly as he could without his teeth, "I think a lot of you dear!"

"What?" she said, squeezing her eyes, half in irritation, worrying that she would lose her count.

"I think a lot of you dear!" he said, more loudly.

"What?" she said, squeezing her eyes more tightly, looking off to the side.

He moved over close to her ear, and in the most compelling voice of which he was capable he said, "I think a lot of you dear!"

As she raised herself up from her chair to go to her bedroom, she squeezed her eyes and threw her head in a quick gesture toward him, "I'm gettin' sick of you too!" she said.

Cold Rage

The barn thermometer read twenty-five below zero when Boris Voros hitched Ted and Sonja to the big grain wagon at 7:30 a.m. He had waited impatiently for a week while a forty-five below zero temperature had paralyzed Saskatchewan. Now he'd go to town for the new pump waiting at the railway station. He snuggled down in the hay he had piled into the deep wagon to cushion the new pump against the bumpy road. He found out how easy it was to break cold cast iron when he tapped the old pump with the hammer to loosen the ice as he poured hot water down it.

He hated the dirty slough water he dipped from a hole chopped through two feet of ice. The cows would barely touch it, and their milk had dried up. It stunk when he heated it on the stove, and the tea tasted terrible. 'Life without good tea wasn't worth a damn,' Boris kept muttering to his wife.

In his fur coat and Russian hat he looked like a big bear hibernating deep in its den. He stuck his head out occasionally to urge the horses along. "You get from the new pump fresh water first before anybody," he told them in his broken English, as their nostrils jetted steam into the cold air. They could drink their fill even before he took a pail to his wife, he promised them. Three times he sucked in large mouthfuls of cold air, tasting it like he'd soon taste the fresh, cold water from the new pump.

There'd be no more of the 'twice-a-day' rages he kept slipping into, once each morning when he chopped the ice to get the slough water, once each noon hour when his wife blamed him for having to use the foul-smelling water in her gravy. His quick temper had resulted in his sleeping alone for the last three weeks. He'd be glad to get the new pump he ordered from Eatons' catalogue. You could always depend on Eatons!

At the railway station he signed his name, then shoved the loosely-bound package deep into the hay. He turned the horses around, telling them it wouldn't be long now...they'd soon have their reward! When he reached home he found the package had broken open. He quickly gathered the parts, but he could find no pump handle. He flew into a rage, and he cursed Eatons as he stamped toward the house. He grabbed a pencil and paper.

"You damn fools!" he wrote, "How the hell you think I get water with no pump handle? What the hell you think I do for cows, you stupid fools! No water for cows, no milk for children! You crazy bastards!" His hand shook so violently he had to stop writing. He'd finish the letter in the morning before the mailman came.

In the early light of dawn he searched the wagon again. Deep in the hay, under the edge of an old binder canvass covering the floor cracks, he spotted the red tip of the handle. He rammed his hand down and grasped it, then headed for the house to tell his wife, whistling as he went. He was about to tear up the letter when his wife criticized him for being careless in the previous evening's search of the wagon. Again he slipped into a rage. He grabbed a pencil and plunked himself down with the letter. He thought about what he had written the night before. "Since I wrote that," he scribbled, "I found handle...but go to hell anyway!"

Merry-Go-Round

Jim Carlson wasn't much interested in the Art Exhibit at the Agricultural Museum, or anywhere else for that matter. In fact, he didn't even know why he had signed up for the Fall Session of Art Classes the College was sponsoring in the Buttonwood Village High School. Maybe it was because anything else they were offering interested him less. He had heard a couple of women discussing the Art Courses at the registration tables. They sounded more enthusiastic than the people registering for other courses. They had talked about the teacher's being knowledgeable about some 'Group of Seven' and 'Old Masters' and such. It meant nothing to him, but he had kept listening and he decided while still smarting from what the doctor said about his lingering depression, when he cut off the pills.

"There are lots of good things out there, Jim," the doctor had told him as he ushered him rather hastily through the door. "And there are lots of good people. Get out there and see what they're up to. Find out why they're out there and not in here. There's not much happiness in pills!"

"My name is Kristli Bannerman," the teacher said, when they had all found places at the art tables. "I'm happy to see there are still people interested in Art!" She'd be about thirty-seven, ten years younger than himself, Jim thought when he first looked at her. Her eyes seemed strangely hard, perhaps even a little angry when she looked down at the class. But her voice was pleasant.

In the second lesson the following week the teacher suggested that those who had little or no interest in art might still find a place in another course. Jim thought she might be referring to him. He quickly began to apply the pencil to the sheet in front of him in a clumsy attempt to sketch something that had a recognizable form. In the third lesson she told him, "It's a real improvement. I'm not sure that barn would stand up to a storm! However, it's a start. Very important -- sketching." She smiled at him a little, and her eyes didn't seem so hard when she was up close.

It was at the end of the fourth session she said she hoped they would all view Bradford Swain's Exhibition at the Agricultural Museum the following Saturday. She wasn't sure she liked his work much, with the distorted landscapes, the mixing of styles and the strange use of colours. But they might all learn something from him, she said. And it would be nice, especially for her -- she being a city girl, if someone from the group could help her understand how the old farm machinery worked. She had heard that some of the old machines were virtual works of art. When all the women in the class looked in his direction Jim felt cornered and he volunteered.

The task he awarded himself turned out to be more pleasant than he had anticipated. Kristli Bannerman's enthusiasm seemed to loosen him up, and he found himself talking freely, almost carelessly, in describing the functions of the machines. She even touched his hand a few times when she laughed at something he said. He told her he would be uncomfortable viewing the Art Exhibit. He excused himself. She would be meeting her sister Elizabeth by the merry-go-round at half past eleven, she informed him. She started to leave, then hesitated.

"There will be someone else," she said. "I'd like to have you meet him. Perhaps we could all have lunch together."

Now Jim Carlson stood by the old horse-drawn manure spreader. He thought of the time at the auction sale when, as a kid, he had watched a politician jump up into the spreader and say that it was the first time he had spoken from a Tory platform! After an uncomfortable silence someone far back in the crowd shouted, "Shove her in gear, Mitch, she's got a good load in her now!" He stood for a moment with his arm resting on the weathered boards of the seat, comfortable in the warmth of the memory.

Then other memories demanded to be recognized; the Saturdays in the spring when he had been hired out to pitch manure for the mean farmer. His arms ached when he thought of it. He found himself trying to spit out the pieces of manure straw that got past his lips when the 'poor boy' threw the manure too close and the cold March wind drove it like hail against his face as he was gulping for air. He could still see the farmer unhooking the empty spreader and hooking onto the full machine which he and the 'poor boy' had loaded while the farmer was out in the field. And the horses pulling their guts out trying to break the spreader loose from the black, miring muck of the lower barnyard, their desperate, clawing hooves churning the swilly mess, as the swelled nostrils in their wildly swinging heads snorted steam into the vaporous ammonia of rotting manure. By mid-afternoon his arms were already so worn that the muscles seized sometimes from the weight of the loaded forks. Still the farmer barked orders to have the machine loaded by the time he got back from the field.

"What is it, Auntie?" The small voice brought him back to the present. A handsome, well-dressed young woman was hanging onto a small boy's hand, looking intently at the machine.

"It's obviously some kind of cultivator," she said.

"Bull!" He immediately felt ashamed, unbelieving that he could have said it. It was an expression he had used in connection with the Commons cafeteria-stuffed politicians who railed about the plight of the poor during question periods. It was an expression he used in connection with the slick evangelists selling immortality. But it was not an expression to be used in front of a lady.

The woman frowned. "I beg your pardon?"

"It's the commodity it dispenses," he said, without raising his eyes.

"Sir?" She looked straight at him.

"I'm terribly sorry," he said, still not sure he was fully in control of himself.

"I wish daddy could see it." The boy tugged at the woman's coat, as though she might bring it about if only she would.

"Oh, Richard!" she said, picking the boy up. "It has been two years," she explained. "He was only four."

"Would you like to know how it works?" he asked.

"Perhaps Richard would," she replied, putting the boy down.

"Can I get up on the seat?" the boy asked, raising his eyes to the woman.

"Is it alright?"

"Sure!" Jim Carlson answered, hoisting the boy up. "Now, if you had some horses, we could all go for a ride!" The boy giggled and swayed from side to side pretending he was the driver. Then, satisfied, he held out his arms to be taken down.

He proceeded to tell the woman and child how, when the machine was in gear, (that lever up by the seat) and the horses moved the machine ahead turning the large back gear wheels, the whole floor -- a kind of endless belt of cross slats -- would move slowly toward the back where the spinning, spiked reel would break the material into small pieces, spreading it evenly over the ground behind the machine.

The spinning, spiked reel! Carlson moved his hand to his leg when he thought of it. It was starting to get dark when the farmer told him to take the last load to the back field, muttering derisively that if he wasn't man enough to lift a forkful of manure, maybe he could at least lift the reins! He had almost completed the unloading when an old piece of barnyard board caught in the reel, bringing the machine to a stop. He had just dislodged the board when the horses lurched ahead, spinning the reel, sending the slashing spike into his leg when he fell. As he hobbled toward the seat, the blood spurting from the deep gash below his knee, he caught a glimpse of the dog losing ground to a jack rabbit it had scared up. He pushed the gear lever to 'out' and yelled at the dog to come, then pulled the horses toward the barn before a desperate blackness fell over him, and he slumped across the seat.

Jim Carlson was watching the dog chase a rabbit when he felt something cold on his forehead. Then he heard voices. He couldn't tell if they were talking to him and if they were he couldn't answer. Gradually the voices became clearer. It was a doctor and a nurse -- he was sure of that. And he was aware of a pain so severe that it kept making him black out momentarily.

"I'm worried about the infection," the doctor said. "Three days and no improvement on that leg. We can't give him morphine for the pain, not with that concussion. He's got a good young heart but with so much blood gone he's got nothing much to fight with. We'll have to decide about the leg by Monday."

"I'd like to try my mother's treatment of salt and water if you will let me," the nurse said. "I'll bring in 'Crazy' to help me on the weekend."

"What?"

"'Crazy'. Oh, of course you don't know who I mean -- Elsie! 'Crazy' is her nickname. I called her that when she said she was going to be a nurse, the silly girl. Can you imagine, the three of them; seventeen, fourteen and eleven -- all saying they're going to be nurses? 'Crazy', 'Crazier' and 'Craziest'. Wait till they've smelled as many bed pans as I have!"

"You're in charge for the weekend," the doctor said. "I've got to get around to see the people with the flu. They'll think I'm neglecting them."

"Try to get some nurses out of those beds and back to work," she said. "Isn't it just like those farmers? In here because of their carelessness, when there's so much flu to look after. My husband was the same way...that's why I'm raising the girls by myself." She stopped talking and reached over to rest her hand gently on his arm. Somehow it seemed to help him and even with the terrible pain in his leg he went back to sleep.

"I'm Elsie. I'm your special nurse for the weekend. I'm not really -- I'm just here because of the flu. I'm not even a nurse, but I'm going to be one. And I promise you that I'll never hurt you!" He couldn't keep his eyes focussed for long, but at times he could see her blue eyes clearly. When she talked, he knew she meant every word she said. He wanted to say something to her, but he still could not put words together. "Mom got a cot put in here so I can rest a little between the bathings and replacing the salt and water pads -- dressings! She says there's got to be someone here every time you wake up. It's important she says. Salt and water -- that's what will do it she says. And if it works -- well, they won't have to...Oh!...it's time to start. The water's just right!"

The five years with Elsie were the best five years of his life -- the five years which would have stretched into

95

a lifetime if it hadn't been for the polio. It was all over in a week after the night she woke up frightened and crying. Elsie gone in a week, and the baby she was carrying gone with her. And the people condemning him for letting her stay on that children's polio ward day and night. He couldn't stop her, nobody could. Those little children had to have someone there constantly, she said. Otherwise they would give up. The twenty years without Elsie had been lonely years.

"Sir! Sir?" He could feel her arm under his lending a degree of support. "Are you ill?" It was a few moments before he could bring himself to answer.

"I'm sorry," he said, struggling to bring himself out of it.

"I was just about to call for help when you went rather rigid and wouldn't respond to my question. But I am a nurse. I decided I would handle it."

"A nurse?" For a moment he saw Elsie in her white uniform. Then, as the vision faded it struck him that some of the characteristics of the woman he now faced seemed familiar. "Let me introduce myself," he said. "I'm Jim Carlson."

"I'm Elizabeth," the woman said, quickly reaching out to catch the hand of the impatient boy. "Now, if you feel alright, we'll go. I would like to see all the displays in the museum, if possible, before lunch."

It was precisely eleven when Kristli Bannerman stepped out of the gallery. She walked towards the merry-go-round with her light coat open to the freshening breeze.

"I wish you could have come along," she called from a distance when she saw Jim Carlson waiting. "I felt the need to discuss a couple of the paintings with someone. I must admit that at one time I thought Swain's paintings might be a bit of a joke, but now I don't know that they are. She turned her eyes toward the merry-go-round.

"I used to think the colours and the grotesque expressions on some of the horses faces were a kind of joke. Look at the one the little boy is riding -- the pain on the horse's face. Have you ever seen anything like it?"

"Maybe -- a long time ago."

"The poor thing, tied forever to the merry-go-round." She became quiet and her face took on a contemplative look. "It may have all started at the merry-go-round -- my interest in Art, I mean. I was four. My mother put me on a horse and suddenly the world was going by with all its colours and shapes. When we speeded up the shapes became distorted, and frightening. I fell into my mother's arms and closed my eyes, and I was safe."

"I'm sorry I didn't go with you to the gallery," he said. "I guess I thought it would be too intimidating. I wouldn't know how to interpret the paintings."

"It's very often difficult to know what the artist is attempting to say. For instance, there's one painting where a young woman is alone at a well. There are some unmistakable lines of the old masters, yet it is somehow contemporary. The woman has drawn a bucket of water, but in cranking the windlass the waist-cord of her garment has become entangled with the rope and she is held fast, just out of reach of the fresh, cool water. She watches, helpless, as the frayed rope is about to pull apart and drop her bucket into the well. Her eyes are fiercely strange. Desperation? Defeat? As I stood there trying to discover what the artist had in mind a sudden shock raced up my spine. It was as though lightning had struck my back brace. At that instant a strange question was hurled at me -- a question demanding to know if I was that woman!" Jim Carlson could find no way to respond to what seemed to be, indirectly, a question to him. He dropped his eyes to the ground and stood uncomfortably scraping the toe of his boot back and forth across the gravel path. When she saw his predicament she quickly changed the subject.

"Do you remember when I talked a little about perspective and form in the third lesson?" She looked across to the limestone cliffs where a few autumn reds and yellows were already darting amongst the mellowing hardwood greens. "Colour -- Form -- Proportion -- Perspective."

"I don't think I ever saw it all together before," he said.

"We sometimes say it's looking at art with a clear eye. It can be a bit puzzling when you try to interpret life that way," she added. She slipped her hand under her coat and shifted her brace. "A little uncomfortable," she said, her face flinching slightly. "Fortunately, I can take it off at night. Eventually I'll be free of it, I believe."

"I'm sorry," he said, quickly checking his hand -- a hand that still remembered reaching to comfort Elsie when she came home those mornings after working all night at the hospital. He had almost forgotten the feel of the sure, strong curve of a woman's back.

"My husband didn't survive the crash. I escaped with only a nagging injury. They tell me my eyes sometimes don't hide it very well!"

"Mommy!" The small boy's excited voice burst through the sound of music and he came running to her.

"I'd like you to meet my son, Richard," she said.

"I believe we've already met," he said, smiling at the boy.

"And Auntie Elizabeth, too," the boy informed his mother.

"I wondered what it was that made you keep looking at me in that strange, questioning way," Elizabeth remarked. "Now I'm beginning to understand."

"It was the similarity in the eyes that made me curious," he said.

"Elizabeth and I are twins," Kristli stated. "But it's seldom that anyone recognizes us as sisters."

"Perhaps I was looking at Art with a clear eye!" he joked.

"Let's have a ride, Richard," Elizabeth suggested, quickly whisking the boy away and onto a horse.

Kristli Bannerman followed the horses to a stop. "My mother used to say, 'When there is no music, it's time to get off the merry-go-round!'" She turned and looked directly at Jim Carlson, her eyes intense, questioning. He could offer only a slight smile as he pondered the meaning of her words.

He swung his gaze to the Escarpment, but he did not see the limestone cliffs, for he was in a big park by the river on a beautiful spring day with his arm around Elsie. After the graduation exercises she came to him in her sparkling white uniform and he slipped the ring on her finger. She cried a little, then a look of wonder came to her eyes, a look that told him she loved him and she would love him as long as life would last. In his heart he was telling her that he would love her forever. They had stolen away from the others and she had kissed him. There was a magic about it that sent great chords rolling through him. That night she gave herself to him for the first time and they openly pledged their love for life.

For life! It was for life! Suddenly it was all made clear. It had been a pledge for life; not a pledge which went beyond life. Elsie would never have thought of such a foolish thing!

Jim Carlson turned back to the intense, questioning eyes fixed on him....

A Promise Made

Val Bateman sat quietly on the flower-decked platform in front of Mt. Holden Hospital waiting for the graduating nurses to line up. It had been a long time since she marched up on that platform to get her diploma -- forty-five years to be exact. At the thought of that day, and what had happened in the next four years, a sweat broke out on her forehead. She lifted the brim of her wide, white hat and wiped away the perspiration with the back of her glove. Unconsciously she let her fingers slide down to caress her right cheek. She quickly realized what she was doing and dropped her hand to her lap. Tears came unexpectedly to her eyes. It was as though they were designed to wash away the thoughts of those terrible years. She would at last be done with it all. But the promise she had made still tugged at her insides. Were the tears just an expression of the hopelessness of it all? How could she go back to that hellish place for the dedication of a new memorial?

She slipped her handkerchief back into her silver purse and shifted to quiet her trembling thighs just as the ceremony began. She knew all of the graduating nurses -- most of them well enough to be her daughters. How beautiful they looked in their white uniforms! She had been beautiful on her graduation day. Just before rushing out to the platform she had looked at herself in the mirror, teasing the last bit of rich, red hair into place. The strangely-blue eyes looking out at her from the mirror reflected such confidence she could scarcely believe they were her own. They seemed to say that she was ready, no matter what direction the road ahead would take.

The girls standing so proudly before her now wouldn't be scattered across the world by a war. They'd have a chance for happiness and children.

She was still a student when they carried the tall, young man in through a blinding sandstorm. 'A mining engineer from Sydney. His name is Frank Dunlop,' the ambulance man said. 'He lost his footing in the storm and fell from the headframe. He's all yours now!'. She looked over at the room where she had washed the caked blood and sand from his body as he lay unconscious. 'Concussion,' the doctor said. 'Internal injuries...a lot of blood gone.'

It was silly, they told her, to talk to him all those times as he lay in a deep sleep for three weeks. She thought he might hear her if she said the right things. Even though he wasn't awake, he seemed to be her friend. When she thought she felt him squeeze her hand a little she screamed and ran into the hallway shouting that he was getting better. She was embarrassed later. 'Keep a little of that enthusiasm for others on your ward,' the matron said. She had not been very successful at that. Certainly not after he opened his eyes ever so slightly the first time and uttered three garbled words. She thought he said, 'Who are you?'

'I'm going off duty now,' she told him. 'I'll be back soon!' His eyes fluttered, then closed. She stood at the door and watched him for a few seconds, waiting for her thumping heart to settle down.

"Only the tough could survive in this outback," Frank remarked, as he sat by the window in his hospital room watching a sand storm blot out the sun.

101

"We are tough," Val said. "Well, tough perhaps doesn't describe what we are. Let's say we're hardy and resourceful!"

"Why anyone would put up with this heat and sand is more than I can understand. There's nothing that would keep me here. I can't wait for the contract to end. Sydney, now that's my kind of life -- where there are real trees and water!"

"We have water!"

"Do you call those muddy reservoirs you drink from, water? I'm talking about the beautiful, deep-blue water of the ocean." He paused and looked over at her. "A bit like your eyes," he stated, half seriously. "Not many sheilas with eyes that colour, I reckon."

"Have you...do you know...many?"

"Sheilas? Of course. The streets are full of them! They're not for me -- not until I get a bit of money around me. I just graduated eight months ago."

"I still have four months to go," she informed him.

"Val...Val! The Governor is almost here," Elizabeth whispered. "We had better get up. He'll likely say something about our retirement. You know, the sad old tune!"

"I must have drifted away."

"Are you worrying again about that date with Casey?"

"It is troubling," Val said. "I know it will be the same question!"

"Sh!" cautioned the master of ceremonies.

This would be the last time she'd have to listen to pompous governors and politicians, Val told herself. After this day her life would be her own -- to do whatever she wished with it.

As the ceremony neared an end the Governor pulled himself up straight and swung his head from side to side casting a broad smile across the audience.

"Today, I have the honour and privilege to carry out one of the most pleasurable assignments of my career. That task is to inform you that Valerie Bateman has been appointed to the National Museum. She is the only woman to have received this great honour!" After the applause subsided he added, "You all are knowledgeable of the wartime exploits of this remarkable lady!"

Wartime! Yes...it was wartime when she graduated. And she was immediately recruited for the National Service in the South Pacific. After two months of intensive training her group was advised that they'd be going to Singapore. Frank would be with the Army Engineers attached to Strategic Hospital Services. Two weeks before they were to leave, she had prepared a picnic supper and they had driven out to the reservoir to watch the kangaroos coming to drink at dusk.

"Damn!" Frank said suddenly. "I've always threatened to take a dip in this big billabong. It's now or never, because I'll be heading for Sydney in a week to help get the ship ready. What do you say?"

"About what?"

"About a swim."

"I have no suit," she said.

"That's no problem here. Damn suits just inhibit your freedom, anyway!"

She hesitated. "If you promise.... Oh, hell! What am I talking about. Let's go!" She ran toward the water scattering her halter and shorts as she went. She bet him that she could stay down longer than he could, then pulled him under before he was ready. When her burning lungs forced her to the surface he was waiting. He reached out and drew her to him, kissing her repeatedly as she tried to get her breath.

"I give up!" she said between gasps. "I won't do it again!"

"You're not through yet!" he said, pulling her toward the shore. He put her down in the shallow water with only their heads and shoulders exposed. He kissed her tenderly, then his ravenous lips came down hard on her mouth, and she in impulsive surrender to the raging forces within her rose to meet him. When it was over he held her close while his fingers lightly traversed her perspiring forehead in gentle caresses.

"I love you, Val," he said, simply. "I can't tell you why, but I think I loved you the moment I opened my eyes in the hospital. I tried not to let my emotions tangle me up, because my head was all wrapped up in plans for Sydney." She began to tremble, and he urged her closer to him. What was this devastating force sending the blood boiling into her brain, she questioned; this power which was taking control of her, driving out innocence and simplicity and sweeping her irretrievably into some strange, new dimension?

"Val? What is it?" Frank asked, struggling to interpret the intense look which suddenly appeared in her eyes.

"Would you die for love?" she asked.

"What a crazy notion! Why did you ask me that?"

"I don't know, really," she said, pondering her own question. "Nothing like that ever entered my mind until a young woman asked me that very question at the hospital. She had just taken an over-dose of sleeping pills. She fled the city and came home after her young husband was shot dead by a robber. She's not in the clear yet. Maybe she'll never be."

"What a strange paradox, when you think of it," Frank stated seriously. "People die for causes. But for love? Maybe it's the same thing. That's something I've never bothered to explore."

She put her lips up close to his ear. As the light breeze sent the warm water rippling over them she whispered, "I love you, Frank!"

"It's settled then," Frank said, after their passion had subsided. "One more dip before we turn it back to the kangaroos, and then...well...."

When they got to the car he slipped a ring on her finger. "We're mates now," he said, squeezing her hand a little. "We're in this together, for thick and thin, for good and bad!"

"Val! Val, you must reply to the governor!" Elizabeth reminded her.

"I...I don't know...I'm honoured...but I'm afraid...you see...I can't accept the appointment. I have a previous commitment. Please excuse me. Thank you, Sir!"

"Val, what the hell is going on in your mind?" Elizabeth said sharply, as they were leaving the platform. "Are you entertaining that crazy notion again, of going back to those horrible places?"

"It's somewhat of an obligation."

"Obligation, hell! It's craziness and you know it when you're in your right mind occasionally! And Casey begging you to marry him. A gentle, loving man like Casey -- how many are there like him? And with plenty of money, too!"

"I'll discuss it with him at dinner. Perhaps we can settle it. But now I'd like to take a walk around the nursery, Elizabeth. Would you accompany me?"

"Of course! My daughter is on duty in the ward this afternoon. She'll be happy to see us."

"It's my last chance to hold one of them."

Val picked up the last few things from her office and started along the jacaranda-lined street toward her home. She felt her feet almost float over the thick carpet of blue petals which had showered down to the sidewalk since morning. She stopped and nudged the petals away with the side of her foot making an open circle for two, exactly as she had done when Frank came to meet her on her graduation day. A peculiar warmth began throbbing in her breast. For a few moments it held her in a state of mild paralysis. Then, as it began to wane, she lifted her eyes to watch the last few petals drift down into the circle. Through the now-empty spaces in the tree tops she could see the hill two miles away where a cloud of red dust rose from the base metal mine. The mine that kept the small city alive. The mine that fuelled the war effort with strategic metals when the Japanese were overrunning South-East Asia and bombing Darwin.

The tension grew each day at Singapore as they waited for the evacuation order while base after base tumbled before the merciless onslaught of the Japanese armies. When the midnight order to evacuate came, Major Iris Dolson routed the nurses from their beds and quickly organized the operation to get the wounded aboard ship. When morning came, the ship-load of casualties with fifty nurses and thirty soldiers was tucked snugly against the steep cliff of a small volcanic island. They would stay there until dark and then make a run for it.

They darted in and out amongst the islands of the Riau Archipelago for three nights as Japanese planes criss-crossed the sea. The off-duty nurses came up on deck at night for relief from the stench of vomit in the blacked-out ship. On the last night, as she and Frank lay in a lifeboat above the wounded and dying, he told her that she had been his only love and would always be his only love, no matter what happened. She rolled into his arms and in the ecstasy of those moments she promised him there would never be anyone but him.

The captain's urgent voice broke from the speakers in the early dawn -- planes approaching! Now the ship shuddered under the thrust of propellers churning at full speed. Suddenly three Japanese torpedo bombers roared over the top of an island and swooped down on the vessel, releasing their torpedoes before the two light anti-aircraft guns fore and aft could get a shot away. Water poured through gaping holes in the ship's sides and the order to abandon ship came immediately. Frank shoved her into the lifeboat with the others as the ship began to heel. Then he scrambled into the boat and guided it as it scraped its way down the twisted hull to the water. The other two lifeboats became separated from them in a heavy monsoon storm, and they were not seen again. In the early morning of the second day they could see Bangka Island, and they made for shore. The twenty nurses and fifteen soldiers waded up onto the quiet beach. Suddenly a wave of Japanese soldiers poured out of the dense jungle with rifles ready. They ordered the men to march down a thick canopied path, and soon their screams pierced the jungle as bayonets spilled their guts on the forest floor. Then the rattle of machine guns...then silence.

"Whores!" yelled the Japanese commander, as he came out of the jungle flanked by soldiers. "Bow to Japanese commander!"

"You tyrannical bastard!" Major Dolson shouted. "Australians will never bow down to you!" Some day *you'll* die for this!" The Commander strutted over to her and brought his baton down across her breasts. "Respect Japanese Commander!" he screamed hysterically. "Line up facing water!" When two nurses started to cry Major Dolson called out firmly, "Hold your heads high, girls. You're soldiers -- Australian soldiers!"

"March!" ordered the Commander. "Fire!" came the command when the nurses were knee-deep in water. It was the last thing most of them heard, for a deafening volley of rifle fire slammed into their defenceless bodies hurling them forward, some lifeless when they hit the water, some to suffocate as their unconscious bodies sucked in the sea. When there was no sign of life, the soldiers returned to the jungle.

As her mind cleared after a bullet through her lung had driven her down, Valerie Bateman found herself propped against another body with only her nose and mouth above the water. A searing pain tore at her chest as she gasped for air. I've got to live, she told herself. I must...tell what happened! As the ebbing tide tugged at her she dug her fingers into the sand and pulled herself up onto the beach before collapsing. When she awoke she was on her back in shallow water. She lay for a while on the silver strip of beach listening to the night sounds as the warm water of the incoming tide rippled across her torn breast. Then she crawled on hands and knees to a coconut tree at the edge of the jungle and leaned her head against its trunk. In the morning she reached for some empty coconut shells and waited for the monsoon rain. As she raised the shell to drink she heard something in the foliage close by. She listened...waited...then turned her head slowly toward the noise.

"They thought I was dead," the soldier whispered in a half delirium, struggling to stay on his hands and knees. She used his knife to cut open a coconut and gave him the milk. He was soon asleep, his bloodied head cradled in her arm. In the morning he was gone. Later that day she heard some excited voices in the distance, then two shots. For the next eight days she hid near the edge of the jungle, going down to the beach in the evenings and early mornings to bathe her wounds. On the tenth day she was awakened by a Japanese soldier's rifle barrel jabbing her in the ribs.

"English bitch," the soldier called, "Walk!" He motioned her toward the beach where a patrol boat was waiting off shore.

Those three and a half years in the prison camp were years of hell. Soldiers died from dysentery on the dirt floor; women with wasted bodies fought like tigers for morsels of food as babies perished at their dried-up breasts; emaciated old men tore at each other's faces over the slugs they scooped from the drains. The suicides...the executions.... It all seemed like a terrible dream now, as Valerie Bateman sat at her kitchen table looking again at the invitation to the dedication of the new memorial on Bangka Island. The radio was playing a song from South Pacific: If you try...you will find me...come to me...come to me.... How many times, as she lay recuperating in the hospital, had those words sent her tortured mind back to that jungle where Frank and the other soldiers were butchered and bulldozed into a mass grave.

Suddenly it was easy to decide. She picked up the phone and called Canberra. "Yes," she said defiantly, "I'll go!"

When the ceremony was over and the politicians were through talking about forgiveness and understanding, she stepped down from the reviewing stand and walked slowly toward the beach where children played noisily on the clean, white sand. They ignored her as she sat quietly under a coconut tree watching them. In the late afternoon, when most of the children were gone, she removed her shoes and walked slowly toward the water, stopping at the edge as three children with curious faces stared at her. She smiled at them and waded slowly out until she was knee deep. She hesitated and listened. Only the sounds of the sea and the faint voices of children now touched her ears. As she moved forward in a slow march the rising water pressed her light dress tightly against her thighs...and the water stung her when she bled that first time and he told her he loved her and she pulled him back into the water and he held her hands and they sank down deep and his voice came in musical waves...I love you...until all the air was gone and they surfaced and did it two more times and the water is at your flat belly where he patted you the second time at the reservoir and he said it would make a good pouch but it never held a baby inside it and now the water is at your half breast where the bullet tore away the nipple and it was all scar and it could never suckle a baby and now the water is at your face where they broke your jaw and it was always crooked and now you are crying and the tear salt is in your mouth and the sea is washing over your lips like the reservoir water that second time when the light breeze sent the delicate waves over you and you stand on your toes and take a deep breath and shout to the world goddam that Japanese commander...goddam war...goddam fate...and the children are yelling at you from shore and you breathe deeply and let your toes slip off the ledge and your body falls forward and your blue eyes are the colour of the ocean at Sydney he said and some day you'd live with the children near the beach and the water is darker than your eyes and there is no more air and you are very deep and your body is a ball and your heart is pounding in your ears in the reservoir and he said I-I-I-lo-uh-uh-h-h-h....

Bittersweet

"I thought I'd see you in the parade, Frank," Nate said, as he sat down for the Legion Luncheon.

"I can't keep up anymore," Frank replied. "The leg, you know -- it's been balking a bit the last couple of years. I couldn't even hobble back to get the bittersweet for Maria this year. She'll be expecting it when she comes by this afternoon. You couldn't go and get it for her could you? It's real important to her, you know."

"I've promised to go to the Reserve to help with the ceremony there. They're short of flag-bearers."

"Are you doing it for Tommy Stonefish?" Frank asked.

"Maybe."

"The best bittersweet is back by the railroad, but you've got to walk through that deep ravine to get there," Frank explained. "It should be nice and red and plump this year with all the rain, and no hard frost yet. That bittersweet's got the reddest berries I've ever seen. It seems to be a special kind, different from the ordinary -- maybe a mutation or something. I wish I could get back there to get it, but this leg won't do it." He looked down at the short leg with the turned-in toe and massaged the knee for a few seconds.

"I wouldn't have this leg if it hadn't been for that woman doctor," Frank said. "They were going to take it off after I got it caught in the cable when we were unloading in Murmansk. We were hurrying to get out of there before the next raid and I slipped on the snowy deck and fell into the hauser. She wouldn't let them take it off. She put it together somehow. Think of that...because of that woman doctor I've had my leg all my life." It was a familiar story, but Nate was willing to listen to it again after ten years, for Frank still showed the need for the assurance which came with telling it.

It had seemed too nice a day for November 11, Nate thought, as he turned the car toward the small town of Buttonwood. The sun was bright, the sky was clear, and it wasn't cold -- not at all like the raw, overcast day you expected November 11 to be.

He had enjoyed the early drive from the city in the comfort of his car, with the radio playing World War II songs. Now as he approached the Legion he grew apprehensive. Would they resent his old air force uniform being stuck in the column amongst their grey flannels after his years of inactivity? When he thought about it, he couldn't determine why he had wanted to wear it. And he wasn't even sure why he wanted to march in the parade after an absence of ten years. Maybe it was for Glen; maybe it was for Maria. Her letter pointed out that it would be the 30th anniversary of the November 11th on which the telegram came -- the telegram which spelled out the message that Glen had died in a bomber over Berlin. The ten years since the 20th anniversary had done little to diminish his sense of loss.

The column was already formed when he pulled the car to a quick stop. He slipped into a spot with the other seven men, just as the old sergeant major pulled himself up straight and rapped his heavy cane on the stones. He swept his cold eyes down the length of the column.

"By the left, Quick March!"

The confusing command got some started off on the wrong foot, and there was a shuffling of worried feet as they searched for the beat of the drum. Some, in whom the piper's call signalled an old message, tried to recall to their steps the youthful precision which had once been theirs. That precision now belonged to the contingent of Girl Guides who stepped out in front to the lilt of the pipes.

Nate glanced over at the seven men whose uncertain feet slapped the pavement in uneasy rhythm, bouncing their bent shoulders up and down, their eyes never quite reaching the horizon. Why had he come back? Was it to tell them that he was still one of them, that the war-welded bond was still unbroken? -- a bond more important now as the years kept taking their strength. And why had the women in the parade come in numbers outstripping the men? To perform a duty? To tell the world that they had been a part of it, and that they still cared and would always care? Did they have a bond which only they could understand -- a bond which would not be easily broken now or ever? For whatever reason in their hearts, they were there to march; some serious, some proud, some with looks of longing in eyes that had grown old alone.

The parade came to an uncertain halt at the Cenotaph where the Silver Star mother from the Indian Reservation stood waiting to honour a husband and a son -- two men taken in war.

The weight of the medals pulled at the forward pitch of her frail form, but her face still showed traces of the strength which had taken her through two wars, wars which for her had lasted most of a lifetime. She gently placed the wreath as the small band of onlookers watched. Some older faces told of the sadness in hearts at that moment, some told of indifference. Some children tried to keep from laughing. Some children tried, in the few silent seconds, to imagine grandfathers who had never been more than a few letters cut into a cold column of stone.

At eleven o'clock a fierce whistle screamed at the silence as a train roared past the open space where the station once stood -- the station from which so many had left; the station to which so few returned; the station in which the dots and dashes of Morse code slowly spelled out words saying the others would never return.

"I told Maria the bittersweet would always be hers when I took over the farm," Frank said. "The place was too much for her alone when Glen didn't come back. She'd miss the bittersweet, she said. That last time he was on leave they walked back there and when she told him she was going to have a baby he hugged her for a long time. Then he said if it was a girl he'd like to call her Bittersweet, because he liked the bittersweet so much. When the girl was born, she couldn't call her Bittersweet, but she called her Holly because it was a real name and it would still have the red berries in it. She thought he'd like that." Frank was silent for a moment and his face grew more serious.

"Things seemed different then. All they wanted was just to live out their lives in peace. That's all any of us wanted. But we went to a war which we didn't understand. And the padres and preachers thanked God on Sundays for our victories -- victories in which a thousand of the enemy were killed for a loss of only five hundred of our men. We didn't know it then, but now it seems to me that we were all part of a mass human sacrifice by competing tribal priests! 'Peace on earth...Good will toward men!' What men? The Germans? They'll be gathering today too -- the ones who can hobble to their meeting places!"

"They're calling the volunteers for the Reserve ceremony," Nate said, interrupting Frank. "I'll bring back the bittersweet."

He didn't know why he had volunteered to help with the ceremony on the Reservation. He thought he might be doing it for Tommy, his boyhood friend, who had died a month earlier from gangrene in an old war wound.

114

But maybe it was because he had some feelings which demanded to be recognized -- feelings which he could not completely identify, but which seemed closer to the surface now than they had ever been. He walked to the Cenotaph with the Indian women and the two remaining Indian men. As the honour guard lowered the flags and the pipes wailed, it suddenly struck him that he wasn't there just for Tommy. He was there for all the Indians who fought and died for their country, a country for which Indian blood and white blood had spilled together, a country which was the Indians' country only during the war and which was snatched away from them again when the war ended and they went back to the Reservations. He wanted to go over and put his arms around the Silver Star mother who now wept silently by the wreaths. He wanted to tell her that he cared. Instead he gently took her hands for a few moments, then turned toward the car.

The Legion was noisy when he returned; noisy with stories driven by blood warmed with nostalgia and wine - - stories of standing with Montgomery in North Africa; stories of a comrade's death in an heroic act of patriotism; stories of acts not so heroic, of brutal barbarism on both sides -- stories only half true. But it did not matter, for events producing such stories are always clouded. The Hong Kong stories were missing now, for there was no one left to tell of the hateful days of the prison camps, yet in the hearts of some who had heard those stories there still lingered hate -- hate quiet until alcohol fired the flames once more.

The raucous atmosphere of the Legion disturbed Nate somewhat. Still, it felt good to be with them again, for amongst those few men and women there was a particular warmth and generosity which had survived the years and could be found nowhere else. It was a place where it was alright to have feelings. A place where people understood -- perhaps the only place after thirty years.

After the two World War I veterans had been duly honoured at the five o'clock banquet, the mayor rose to speak. He turned slowly to the two old soldiers and hesitated, seeming not to know what to say. Then he took a nervous breath and began.

"We are here to remember," he said haltingly, "and to honour our men and women who have served our country in the cause of peace. We are not here to glorify war. We have had enough of war! When we remember those who did not come back to us, it should be an emotional experience. If it is not an emotional experience, what is the point of this exercise? Our words are but words ringing with deception, cold and cruel. I don't want such words for those young men and women! I don't want such words for my father...." He could not continue and he turned from the podium.

"It's alright, Jim," Frank said, reaching out to touch the mayor's hand as he quickly edged by the table. "Jim never got over losing his father," Frank stated in a voice subdued with melancholy, as he watched the mayor go through the back door.

At six o'clock Maria arrived and came directly to their table. She took Nate's hand in hers.

"Thanks," she said. "I'm glad you decided to come." Then she turned to Frank. "The bittersweet," she questioned. "Is it...?"

"I came that way when I returned from the Reserve," Nate assured her.

"It's almost time," she said, lifting her watch on a nervous wrist. "Would you like to come?"

"Sure," Nate replied.

"Jim and Holly always seemed right for each other," Maria remarked, as they walked toward the Cenotaph. "Neither of them ever wanted anybody else. He went to that school in London where she was in training at the hospital just to be near her. Maybe it was natural that it should be that way, with their fathers both taken over Berlin in the same plane." It was a moment before she could continue. "I...I never saw two people more in love," she said.

"Maybe I did," Nate remarked calmly.

Maria looked at him with a slight smile and for a few seconds her face glowed.

The sun had gone down leaving the day to grow cold by the time they reached the Cenotaph. Maria opened her bag and removed the small wreath she had made from the wild grape vine. She carefully wove the bittersweet into the wild vine. Then she set her eyes on her watch and waited until 6:17, the time the telegram was placed in her hands on that November 11th so long ago. She put the wreath down softly against his name, letting her fingers hesitate momentarily on the red berries. Then, as her eyes began to moisten, she raised herself and stood quietly erect.

Nate put his arm around her shoulder and lightly touched his face to her cold cheek. When the time was right he moved back from her and let her be alone. She stood for a few moments staring into the distance, her hand gently clasping the sprig of bittersweet she had kept. She lowered her eyes to the red berries as the November darkness closed around them.

"Glen would have been twenty-three in another five days," she stated quietly.

"I always got his birthday mixed up with those of the other kids in our family," Nate said.

Polarquest

It was a strange mix of men perched on the sandbank above that small creek on Melville Island. They were the kind of men whose eyes need space -- young men mostly. Some were chasing adventure, some were running from women, some were looking for wealth, some were seeking solitude, and some, without knowing it, were searching for something within themselves -- something not easily defined. For whatever reason, they were there. Some were there with no reason except that they had to be somewhere.

Being in the Arctic gave some of the men, for the first time in their lives, a purpose and a usefulness which they could not have anticipated. The need for survival in the High Arctic soon imprints itself on a man's consciousness and his instincts direct him into jobs which he would have turned down flat in the society from which he has severed himself. It did not seem unusual then that a young man from Finland, trained as an accountant, should end up as a cook for the twelve men of a seismic exploration crew in the Polar Islands.

"I've got too good a sense of humour!" Armo would say when the men asked him why he wasn't working in accounting. "You know that accountants have no sense of humour. I have, and that's why I'm cooking." Then he'd laugh and pour fresh coffee into their raised cups. They suspected that there was more behind his being in a lonely arctic camp than Armo was disclosing, but there was no thought of pressing him about his past. Instinct tells men in the Arctic to avoid such things. Besides,

Armo was the best cook the camp had had. There was no sand in his pies. He always called them over to the kitchen at ten each night for hot coffee and rolls right from the oven.

"You can write and tell my boss," he'd say sometimes, when they'd thank him for the good food. "Then I'll never have to go back. If I can make anything special for you, let me know. I still have a lot to learn."

"Polar bear stew!" Eric called. "That's what I'd like to try if you can wangle a hunk of meat from the Bathurst Eskimos some day when Dick brings the supplies."

"Buttermilk pop!" Helmut, the old German said. "That's what we called it. I remember it as a kid." He stood pondering for a moment. "I don't suppose anybody in Canada has heard of it. I don't know how they made it. It was a long time ago."

"I'll look for it when I get some time to read. Maybe we'll have a celebration." Armo remarked, prompting a smile in the clear, blue eyes of the aging helicopter engineer.

That night, as every night, they checked the two loaded rifles slung in a handy place by the door, ready if a polar bear should wander into camp. Then they settled into their sleeping bags in the dusky light, as the yellow-orange sun slid sideways along its harmonic wave. And that night, as every night, their talk turned to women for a while before each man was left alone with his thoughts in the sleepless silence.

How easy it was, wrapped in a sleeping bag under the translucent Quonset cocoon so close to the arctic night, to think of women the way they were at eighteen when you first kissed them. They had a freshness, a sweetness and simplicity then. Why couldn't they stay that way? Maybe they would if they didn't get their lives tangled up in the city. Maybe...maybe if.... Then cold reality would interject to tell them that when they went back, the women would be the way they left them; complicated, mysterious, hard to get along with, robbed of the girlish freshness they had wanted them to keep -- robbed of the things which made them exciting and wonderful....

"Time to get up, boys," Armo called. "Breakfast is all ready. Lots of good coffee. I got all the sand out of the creek water this time! If I get breakfast over early enough, Denver is going to take me in the helicopter when he takes the Dane and the lad to put up the radio tower. Maybe we'll see a polar bear. I'd sure like to see one."

Denver swung the helicopter out over the pack ice along the shore and set a course for the spot where they would drop the men off. A few miles from the tower site they spotted a couple of seals lying on the ice in the early sun. Beyond a narrow stretch of water, its nose searching for direction, was a polar bear.

"He's after his breakfast," Denver said. "He intends to surprise those seals. He'll dash across that lead and come up behind the ridges. Then he'll make a great leap over a hummock and knock them out before they can slip down their hole, if he's lucky. An Eskimo told me he saw a bear knock out seven seals one time when he took them by surprise."

"Maybe we'll scare him away," Armo ventured.

"Polar bears are afraid of nothing," Denver stated. "To me, they're the most dangerous animals on earth. If you haven't got a gun there's no chance with them -- not like there is with another bear. There...he's swimming! Now we'll see what he's all about." He brought the helicopter down to within a few feet of the water directly over the bear. Its elevated nose scarcely broke the surface as its wide paws struck out in bold determination thrusting its creamy hulk forward, its back legs trailing straight out behind. They watched in fascination as the great animal moved steadily toward the seals, its greasy coat slipstream slick in the icy grasp of arctic sea.

"He's twelve feet long if he's an inch," Denver remarked. "He'd stand eight feet on his back legs without trying."

"He's a 'she'" the Dane said.

"What?"

"He's a 'she'" the Dane repeated. "I know that bear...I know that bear for sure! Look at the right front paw. The inside toe is missing. And there's a big scar on her nose. It's the same bear, for sure."

Suddenly the bear reared up, churning the frigid sea into foam with its flailing back legs as it lashed out toward the pontoons with extended claws, its jaws snapping open in a defiant display of incisors.

"We'll get out of here," Denver said. "I'd rather that the seals should be his breakfast. How do you know that bear, Dane?"

"It was the day after I arrived from Denmark in early spring to work on my thesis," the Dane began. "I got the job right away because I knew something about towers from the summers I worked in Greenland. We left the Twin Otter down on the beach and the pilot walked up with me to the cliff that morning to find a place for the first tower. We could smell something strange drifting toward us. It seemed to be coming from a snow cave in the shelter of the cliff. Then we saw a bear's head just over the cliff above the snow cave. We were paralyzed with fear as we waited for the bear to come at us. But the bear was watching a little column of steam coming from the cave and we ducked behind an ice sheet hanging from the cliff. Suddenly the bear leapt down onto the roof, crashing into the cave where there was a young female with a cub. The young female struck furiously at the intruder in a magnificent defense of her cub, but she succeeded only in slashing open the attacker's nose before the crushing jaws of the large bear closed on her throat. The battle was over. The great bear killed and ate the cub, then urinated on the dead female before lying down to rest. We sneaked back to the plane and stayed there until the bear went out onto the ice. Then we checked the tracks. They were over a foot wide, all except the right front one that showed the missing toe."

"Well, Armo, you've seen your polar bear and an unusual one at that." Denver remarked.

"And I don't think I care to ever see another one," Armo replied weakly. "Somehow, I thought it would be more of a pleasure."

When Dick put the Twin Otter down on the sandy shore that evening at nine to pick up the Dane and his helper, he found them clinging to a ledge on the steep rock face.

"The bear followed us down this morning," the Dane said. "We just had time to scramble up the cliff. That bear on its hind legs was only three feet away with its slashing claws, and those grinding, guttural growls felt like they could shake the whole cliff down. After three hours, in desperation I threw the sledge hammer. I think I got an incisor in its lower jaw. It went back out onto the ice and we worked till the light started going."

"You'll feel better with some hot grub," Dick offered. "Armo's waiting for you. Now, if we can get this thing off the ground," he said seriously, as he pulled the Otter up from the soggy beach on the third try.

It was an eager band of men who waited for Armo's ten o'clock call for fresh coffee and cake that night. It was always satisfying in the jovial mood of Armo's kitchen. It was a place where the love of good food substituted for a while for the love some of the men had left behind. Armo had become such an integral part of their lives that it was inconceivable to think of a day without him.

"Whose going to take care of us tomorrow?" they called, when Armo said that he might take the new cook books and hike over to the eastern ridge to see what made the strange spectrum of colours for a few seconds every morning, just as the sun broke over the top.

"There's plenty to get you through until I'm back," Armo assured them. "And now I want you boys to show me how to sling the rifle over my back so it will land in my hands when I throw my shoulders forward."

The next morning after the men had gone, Armo slung his pack onto his back and positioned the rifle over it the way they had taught him. He didn't know why Eric at the last minute had shoved the survival sheet into his pack. He'd only be away for a few hours, he argued. Yet he knew that they were concerned about him and it wasn't just because of his cooking. Maybe they were the only people on earth who really cared about him, he thought.

Morning was still extending the edges of the blue arctic dome as Armo stepped over the small stream below the camp. The percussion of his heavy boots striking gravel was the only sound he heard as he started across the gently inclined plain toward the ridge in the early stillness -- a stillness that seemed as real as the land itself. Soon the crystal ping of fracturing shale rang up from his boots, and Armo began to sing to the accompaniment of his expanding orchestra. It was surprising how good his own voice sounded to him. Why does a man sing to himself when he's alone, he questioned. Is it because he is territorial like the birds? Is it right in his genes as a protection against intruders? Is it another verse in his mother's cradle song? At first he sang silly little tunes he made up about the men, but soon his songs about the men dissolved into songs of his homeland. He was a boy in school again...'Dear land of home...our hearts to thee....'

He had not thought of jealousy entering into it when he accepted the top student award at the accountants' graduation. Later at the party, Janna slipped into his arms and kissed him. Then the drunken insults...the argument.... He didn't push the drunken boy from the icy steps, but enough of them lied about it to get him convicted of manslaughter. He escaped, caught a Norwegian freighter to Montreal, then made his way to Edmonton and the accounting job. 'I like your sense of humour,' the chief accountant's wife said at the Christmas party. He had never intended that it should go any farther than that.

What would life have been like in Helsinki, with Janna? Maybe she would be there waiting for him yet. He could still feel her in his arms and taste her lips when she said she loved him. For a moment he felt an almost irresistible compulsion to turn back to camp and pack up for home. He stood for a while half dreaming, half thinking. Then, for the first time in his life the punishing realization came to him. He would never be going back.

He stumbled on disinterestedly until he came upon a muskox skull lying by a shallow rivulet. An old male, he thought, kicked out of the herd because he was too mean. Meeting a violent death when he came to drink. A little below, a few arctic poppies had found a spot in the sterile soil where some nutrients had leached from bones. He stooped down to study them. The small, fragile plants leaned towards the low sun, as if watching for the approach of the long darkness. He thought of their tenuous hold on life as he let his fingers gently caress the petals of two of the flowers. A few inches below them ten thousand years of permafrost still locked the land in cold paralysis.

Suddenly he was aware that he had stopped for some time and the day was slipping away from him. He chose to follow a shorter route up the valley of the small stream. The climb became steeper now and he found himself tiring easily. And the abrasive stones chewed at his boots and bruised the soles of his feet. Twice when he stopped for a minute's rest he thought he heard something, but he put it down to his imagination. Still, he felt a strange uneasiness. He looked back across the wide stretch of barren tundra separating him from the camp. The orange Quonsets looked incredibly small, like miniature shells. He remembered what Denver had told him about distances in the high arctic being dangerously deceiving. He'd be alright when he had his thermos of coffee and the sandwiches at the top, he assured himself. Then he would head back home.

He could now see the sea ice showing over the lower western end of the ridge. The sea and sky had become one. It could mean a storm, he thought. He didn't know what compelled him to do it, but a couple hundred feet from the top he called out Hello! Hello-o-o! came the reassuring reply. He laughed and called out again. Ten feet from the top he spotted some strange looking glass-like rock. "That's it!" he said excitedly, as he picked up some broken pieces. He turned them over in his hands and watched the sun split the light into a strangely confused spectrum of colours. He thought of packing a few pieces but he worried about the weight.

As he stepped to the top he slid his cap off. He threw his head back and let the clear, cold air sink slowly into his lungs as his eyes swung lazily over the vast expanse of sea ice. Suddenly he heard a quick scuffing below him. Then his terrified eyes confronted the charging bear. He threw himself forward and grasped at the rifle but his momentum sent him stumbling over the rock-strewn ground. By the time he had recovered the bear was upon him. It grabbed the rifle butt in its

125

massive jaws and ripped it away. As a cursing Finnish oath poured from Armo's throat the bear's brutal paw struck a blinding blow virtually severing his body at mid-section. Armo was dead before his desperate cry calling throughout the valley had grown to a whisper in the depths of arctic silence.

It was two days later, after the snow storm had abated, that two hunters trailing the bear came in with the rifle, a cook book and the sole of one of Armo's boots. There was nothing else worth carrying, they told the Dane in Eskimo language.

The camp was quiet for several days after that. It was a couple of weeks before the men showed much interest in anything, including food. Then Carl came across one evening from Bathurst, the last fuelling stop for the new helicopter he had brought from Resolute. The excitement of the men, as they gathered around the shiny jet machine the next morning, seemed to point to more normal times ahead.

"What kind of meat was that in your stew, Jim?" Eric asked the new cook after they had finished supper that night.

"Polar bear," Jim replied. "Carl brought it over from Bathurst last night. The Eskimos were celebrating because they finally caught 'missing toe', they said."

"Missing toe?" Eric queried.

"Carl said it was a bear that had terrorized the settlement for a year," Jim explained. "It had killed and eaten some of their dogs last winter when it caught them asleep in the snow. A hunter shot off part of its foot one time, but the bear always seemed to get away."

The Dane jumped to his feet and grabbed the radio microphone, at the same time calling for Armo's rifle. As he examined the deep teeth marks on the stock while talking excitedly in Eskimo, the men sat in wonderment, looking back and forth to each other.

"The teeth marks," the Dane said, holding up the rifle as he hung up the microphone. "The missing incisor -- the one I knocked off with the sledge hammer when the bear chased us up the cliff. It matches their bear! And the tracks they found by Armo's rifle -- a missing toe on the right front foot. It's the same bear!"

The men were already racing for the door, hands clamped tightly over their mouths. Then the sounds of violent regurgitation shook the evening calm as convulsing guts spewed their contents over the sterile sand. Men sank to the ground in moaning, sickening terror.

"Bring what's left, Jim," Eric ordered, when he could compose himself.

They gathered the regurgitated material into a pail and carried it with the remaining stew to a small sandy hill looking out across the barren stretch to the ridge. There they dug a miniature grave eighteen inches deep and emptied the contents of the containers onto the permafrost floor.

Denver waited as the troubled sun broke over the ridge the next morning, then pulled his helicopter into the cold air and guided it across the naked tundra toward a dim display of colours on the ridge. In a half hour he was back with several buckets of strange looking rocks.

"It's an unusual kind of quartz," he said. "It flashes like a beacon when the sun is right."

In a jar inside the cairn of special quartz on Armo's grave they left a note. It gave his name, his place of birth and the date of his death. At the bottom of the note one of the men had scribbled the words:

'A Man's Quest Shall Be His Home'

Down the Right-of-Way

I'm only telling you this because I promised Mac I would, that last night we were all together in the motel. It was my last day on the job. I had planned it that way. But none of us knew that it was to be Kelly's last day.

It had all started for me a year and a half earlier when I ran out of money and had to leave Art School at Christmas. A friend at the school told me that his dad might need a helper on the pipeline. In desperation, I grabbed at the chance and the day after New Years I was on the site as Mac's helper.

"Fire up!" somebody yelled. I watched as Kelly's torch struck steel and the harsh, blue flame flashed against the cold sky of the winter dawn. For a moment I stood transfixed at the beauty and dynamics of the colours and sounds, as Kelly wove his trademark into the molten heat of creation, to be frozen the next instant in the great band of steel.

"Watch how Kelly's helper does it," Mac said, in a half-order. "You've got till noon to get up to speed!"

His words jarred me into the realization of the purpose for my being there. I became aware of the roar of machines as the big cats, snorting under the heavy loads, swung the huge pipes into the right position at the right time.

"Better put this on, you're shaking already!" the large, friendly-faced man said in a mid-European accent, as he handed me a parka. "It's Kelly's extra. He said to give it to you. My name's Mike," he added, as his hand came out of a heavy glove to take mine.

"Shove some rods into that hand and kick his ass in my direction. We've got work to do!" Mac shouted, as my hand slipped from Mike's.

"He's not bad like he sounds," Mike explained. "But you have to work hard, like he does."

Mike was right about that. By mid-morning my Art School muscles were stinging. And my Art School sensitivity was bruised to the degree that I was ready to flee into the bush, to where or what I did not know. When I told Mac that I had to relieve myself and could wait no longer, he lifted the hood from an unsmiling face.

"It's a three-rod deal on this job," he said. "When that third butt slips from my torch, be out of the bush, or you'll get run off the spread!"

When I handed him the rods just as the last red-hot butt hit the ground, Mac lifted his hood and he was smiling. I knew we'd be alright together after that.

Kelly already had a fire going in the shelter of a thirty-inch pipe when we walked up with our lunch buckets at noon. He tossed a light smile in my direction and asked Mac how I was doing.

"He's already toilet-trained. Another three-rod man!" They both laughed -- at my expense, I thought.

"You wasn't that easy on me," Kelly said, "keeping me in that swamp all day."

"Kelly, if I hadn't sprung you, you'd still be pounding rocks. I told them I'd be responsible. I had to get that crazy head of yours straightened out."

"You've made a good start, Mac," Kelly acknowledged.

That night I saw Yvette for the first time. She was sitting by the window as I came through the door to the dining room. Her eyes caught mine and hung onto them for quite a while. Something seemed to go between us, and as I went to the special section where they put our crew out of sight and sound, I could feel her eyes following me. A few days later I talked to her. By that time I knew from the men why she was there. I found out that after business hours she stayed with Surly Strawboss Joe, or S.S. Joe, as the men dubbed him. Nobody had ever figured out why she got hooked up with him. She told me that she left the East when she was fifteen, just after they made her give her baby boy away when she wouldn't name the school-boy father. She had followed the pipeliners ever since.

"You remind me of that little boy," she said in French-flavoured words. Her soft, brown eyes looked straight into mine. "He'd be about your age now," she added, closing her eyes and dropping her head for a moment. I wanted to tell her that I had been given away in Montreal when I was a baby. And at that moment I wanted to tell her that I wished she were my mother, no matter what she was.

Mac told me about you," she said. "He needs a woman to talk to sometimes, so he talks to me. Nothing else. He wouldn't cut out on his wife, even if they don't get along. He's not like the others. But they are my crew, and I take care of them. I'm maybe, one of the crew?" Her laugh did not sound happy.

I had trouble getting to sleep that night. It seemed that I had scarcely closed my eyes when Mac's whiskey-dry vocal chords sounded the new day.

"Out of those bear traps, you guys. It's special events day for Kelly and we'll need your moral support." Mac explained to me that he had a little surprise for S.S. Joe. He opened his bag and there under the ham sandwich and carton of milk, were an old desk phone and an alarm clock. "He's been hard on Kelly lately," Mac said. "Of course, Kelly's not helping much, being ugly half the time from booze and lack of sleep since he's been chasing that little bar maid from the East. The damn fool...running around with everything. That's why his first wife ditched him. She showed up one day after somebody squealed on him about going to the doctor for the shots. He just can't seem to settle down. He'll never have a nickel to call his own."

Mike grinned as we walked to the back of the bus and sat down beside him. The big, affable pipeliner had left Europe at the end of the war a 'skinny runt' he said. He had started to grow again at twenty when he went to work in the nickel mine. He was already a trusted friend of mine. But he was not a friend of S.S. Joe. He couldn't be after S.S. Joe had called him an ignorant bohunk that first day on the job. "I'd have strangled him, but it was a chance to get away from the mine, and I hung onto my head," he explained. "I get the bad jobs, but some day I'll get a new boss, maybe."

S.S. Joe stomped heavily into the bus, swinging his eyes around to count the men, ending on Kelly. Then he turned and sat down. About five miles out when most of the men, including S.S. Joe, were dozing lightly, Mac motioned to Mike.

"It's time," he said quietly, drawing the phone from the bag and slipping it under his coat. Then he reached into the bag and triggered the alarm clock in three loud, intermittent rings. Snatching up the telephone, he said seriously, "Hello! Who? Yeah, he's here."

S.S. Joe grabbed the receiver and was shouting Hello! before he realized it was a hoax. He started to raise his voice in anger, but the laughter of the men drove him to his seat to stare humbly at the floor, while Jimmy, the oldest cat driver, sang tauntingly, "Has anybody here seen Kelly...?"

S.S. Joe let up on Kelly after that and Kelly responded by often volunteering for the dangerous jobs. Kelly was a damn fool, some said. Others said Kelly had a wildness to satisfy and the dangerous jobs were just a part of it.

That summer, after his second divorce came through, Kelly married the woman who worked at the bar. She went back east soon after. He started sending her his pay for the home, and the life they were planning. There were no more bars for Kelly. His life now had a purpose. The overtime and the dangerous jobs -- it all meant money, a home and a good life up ahead.

"Michelangelo should have gotten danger pay!" Mac answered one morning, when Kelly called to him for the 'thought for the day'. The practice had started when Mac was looking for a way to keep Kelly's focus on the positive, after his release from the reformatory. By now the 'thought' had become a regular feature and the men listened for it each morning before tackling the job. That night, when the men were discussing the merits of danger pay, one of the men asked Mac to explain the 'thought' statement of the morning. And that night several of the men learned about Michelangelo for the first time. But Michelangelo could not crowd women out of the conversation for long. And on that night Kelly's new wife came up for discussion.

"What do you think of Kelly's wife, Mike?" someone asked, pressing a reluctant Mike into the discussion.

"Well," he said, "she doesn't look much...how do you say...like a one-owner, low-mileage model!"

When Kelly found out the next morning, he lunged at Mike and his fists flailed against Mike's chest. Mike's big arms folded around Kelly and held him until he settled down.

"I tried to make a little joke," he said apologetically. "I wouldn't hurt you, or her either. I was a fool."

"A damn fool!" Kelly fumed, spinning around and stomping down the right-of-way.

"Mike's hurting a little himself," Mac explained to me. "When he left the mine, a good friend of his said he'd do things around Mike's house to help his wife. But

Mike didn't know his wife would be on the list. He said he hadn't wanted the guy to be that good a friend!"

While we waited for the pipe to be lined up Mac's torch sketched another of his cartoons on a cut-out section of pipe. In his hands the torch became an artist's pencil.

"You should have gone to Art School, Mac," I suggested.

"I wanted to. I could have, too. But I guess I wanted to get married more. In those days your wife didn't work to put you through college." He lifted his shield and looked mischievously at his creation. "You know, I've got a string of these things from the Middle East, through Europe and North and South America. Won't the archaeologists have a hell of a time trying to figure it all out when they dig these up!" He got down on the muck board and crooked his arm into the trench dug under the pipe so two skids would do instead of three, in the interest of economy.

"I'm going to get away from this damn job some day!" he called up to me. "Some day it will be three skids high and down hill all the way." His torch laid a bead of steel as smooth as the raindrops on the pipe above him. I knew he'd never leave the job. Nor would the others, for it was an inseparable part of them. It allowed their kind life; it allowed their kind of language -- a language which cut a path for their thoughts, as surely as the flux cut a path for their torches bonding the steel sinew which snaked across the land, holding the country together.

"You're a natural artist," I ventured, when Mac stood up.

"An artistry that warms people's asses rather than their hearts! And the reward? It's the glory of the cold ground for some like that American tracker in the Middle East, and the young swamper they sent back to Canada in a sealed, lead bag. And the others.... I think about it sometimes...and all the friends I've lost."

"You can work with a pipeliner who has all his fingers -- he's a careful man," Mac stated soberly the next morning when the call came for the 'thought for the day'. It was a serious message and seemed appropriate, because it was easy to become careless in the cold. And it was not a morning for frivolity, for the air was charged with tension lingering from the violence of the previous night.

It came about because S.S. Joe thought Yvette had gone back to drinking again, when he found her staggering and woozy. In a violent outburst of temper he beat her savagely. When she ran to Mike, holding a hand over her battered eye, he sprang through the door like a huge cat to S.S. Joe's room and clamped his great arm around S.S. Joe's throat.

"You bastard! I'll stop you breathing if you ever hit that woman again!" he screamed. When he finally dropped his victim and came back, his whole frame still vibrated in traumatic pulse. "I might have killed him," he said, looking to Mac. Mac poured some whiskey for him.

"It had to be done," he said, reassuringly.

Now, as we watched S.S. Joe walk aimlessly down the muddy, November right-of-way alone, seemingly oblivious to what was going on around him, I wondered how it could have happened.

"That damn idiot!" Mac blurted out. "She's been on strong medication, but she didn't want to tell him. She didn't tell anybody but me. She's real sick. She won't be trading anymore. She's got nothing left to trade."

Within a week Yvette was gone without revealing her departure plans to anyone but Mac. "Tell the boys there will be another 'she-wolf' at their door soon," she said, trying to raise a weak smile, the last time Mac saw her. She was going home to spend the last days. When the letter came from her mother saying it was over Mac told the men as Yvette had asked him to do.

S.S. Joe left the job shortly after that. He was going to see her grave, he said. Following that, he didn't know where he would be -- maybe dead, he thought.

It was a winter of crushing cold and savage storms, and the men dreamt up schemes to wrest their spirits from winter's grip and alleviate the drudgery of the dark days. There was the time six of them walked up hill past twelve horrified visitors from China, carrying an old boot-hill coffin they found in a junkyard. Inside lay Mac, with his hood down. And there was the time they fashioned a substitute shield by cutting a hole in the bottom of an old chamber pot, sticking a welding glass in it to look through. It was cause for some consternation amongst senior officials as they watched with their wives from the cosy cabin of their tracked vehicle.

Mac arranged a visit to an Art Gallery one time, but the curator put an abrupt end to the visit when one of the men, standing amongst the Sunday visitors observing an abstract, called out loudly to the others, "We'd better get the hell out of here before they blame us for that, too!"

With the winter broken, it was time to push forward to the wild tributary of the Fraser. I longed for the day we would reach the river, for it was to be my last day on the job. Now the men faced a serious challenge -- the challenge to get to the river on schedule after major winter hold-ups. Now there was a project which would demand the best from every man in the crew -- a project which would determine their worth. It meant long days and weekend work. It meant the disciplining of tempers if they were to reach their goal. Normal socializing came to a halt as their energy went into the race to the river.

The men were in bed early the evening before the last day. On that day they would lay more pipe than any crew had ever put down in a single day. It would mean a big bonus, and it would mean that they were the best crew in the country.

"Quick, Mac, the thought for the day," Kelly demanded, as the bus stopped at the spread.

"How about this?" Mac responded. "If you're born to drown, you'll never hang!"

They left the bus in high spirits that morning and when the call 'Fire up' rolled down the peaceful valley of early dawn, they were ready to work. By noon the explosives crew was ready to blast the trench in the rocky river bottom, and the helicopter circled to warn away intruders.

"I've volunteered to swamp the last stretch," Kelly said. "It's too risky for the young fellow."

"I thought you got enough swamp the first day on the job!" Mac joked.

"I'll be out of the swamp after this," Kelly replied, soberly.

At three o'clock the big cat swung the boom out and hooked onto the sling Kelly had put around the forty-foot length of pipe. "I'll ride this one for balance," he told the operator. The cat crept over the rocky ledge above the gorge, with Kelly waving it on.

"Stop! Stop!" Mac yelled, when he sensed what was happening. He raced toward the machine, screaming to the operator. But it was too late. With the sound of a rifle crack a piece of the ledge broke loose, flipping the cat onto its side, tearing the pipe from its sling and plunging Kelly into the raging river. The men, stunned and silent, watched the wild water slam Kelly against the rocks, leaving him senseless and broken before turning him loose into the current. When the helicopter snatched him up three miles downstream, his body was lifeless.

Nobody knew why Jimmy drove the cat so close to the lip of the gorge. Some said he forgot to take his insulin that morning. One thing was certain, his mangled hands would never again lend their delicate touch to order into action the big cats he loved.

That night they gathered up Kelly's things. There was a letter from his wife, along with a bank close-out slip. The letter said she was leaving and not to try to find her.

"I got him started," Mac said, as he sat with eyes closed, his hand rubbing his forehead. "I thought he was on his way, but it just seemed that he was always the ragged end of everything."

"The people don't know the cost," Mike said. "It's like in the mine."

"And they don't give a damn!" Mac added. "They'll never know about Kelly."

"Yes they will, Mac!" I said.

I think about it all sometimes when I touch a match to my studio bunsen burner, and watch the capricious, blue flame. I can see Kelly on that first morning, his torch sparking and spitting, blazing into the winter dawn....